MAKING THE GHOST DANCE

One

W hen Peck was eleven and felt invisible, his father, the doctor, brought magic home. It was a surprise. Peck heard his father say to his mother: "Hopefully it will bring him out." There was a silk handkerchief which, when Peck coiled his hand on it, whisked red to green ... then green to red again. There was a wooden egg Peck could make appear and disappear from a red bag on a black stick. There was a deck of cards which, when Peck riffled, forced anyone who reached to pick the jack of hearts. There were two Chinese sticks with tasseled strings which Peck could make dance invisibly. Peck and his father spent the evening together reading instructions, practicing, rehearsing. Everything seemed magic that night. Everything seemed possible. Peck's mother brought fresh-baked cookies and hot cider. And when one of his father's patients called, his father said: "Tell them I'm not available. Tell them Dr. Wyman is on call."

So the message Peck received that eleven-year-old day was that you could start out the day alone, dropping beech leaves into the brook at the Underwood Estate and feeling queer about yourself like a runt animal or freak. Then that night you could be with your family doing tricks and nothing else mattered, everyone you loved would be interested in you and there with you, treating you as if they were you. And words would come into your mouth. You could talk. You could stand at one end of your father's room and fool your parents and they would love you. *Anything was possible.* Peck would never forget that lesson.

Anything *was* possible. Peck started doing magic everywhere. He did it in his room instead of homework. He did in on the back seat of the bus to his music lesson in Cambridge. He stuffed sponge balls into his pockets, filled his sleeves with silks, carried decks of cards. He excused himself to go to the lavatory and changed water into wine in the chipped enamel sink. His mother donated a chewed suitcase as a carrier, and Peck sneaked the suitcase to scout meetings, where instead of learning lashings, he mystified even the Eagles.
"I'm famous," Peck told his mother.
"Be modest," his mother said.
"I'm getting famous," Peck said.
"That's better," she said and pulled Peck so close, Peck believed he could feel her bones trembling. "Don't grow up too fast," she said. "Don't grow up too fast and leave me."

He earned money. He shoveled driveways in winter, delivered papers, made jewelry out of seashells the way he'd learned at day camp and went door-to-door selling. He collected newspapers and scrap aluminum in his cart, bundled and sold them to the junk man. He smudged his face with grease so he looked like Oliver Twist, then sat in a doorway in Harvard Square moaning, crying, begging. One woman gave him forty dollars. When the prospects seemed right, Peck would omit school

from his schedule and sell lemonade or comic books in so
strange neighborhood. His mother had given him an old ca
table for his tricks and he would haul that with him and set
up. One or two weeks—at only twelve now—he made close t
a hundred dollars.

"What are these absences on your report card?" Peck's father, the doctor, asked. "I don't remember that you were ill last
term."

"There's a new lady in the office," Peck said. "She mixes
people up with the same last name."

"Whose grades are these?" Peck's father asked.

Peck looked at the card: three Cs, a D, and a B in English.
"The B's mine," Peck said.

There were stores in Boston that lured Peck to them, one
down an alley, a novelty and joke shop called Humpty Dumpty's. That's where Peck's father had bought the tricks for his
birthday. Every Saturday, Peck took the bus and subway to hang
out in Humpty Dumpty's watching a magician there do tricks.
Peck bought more props. He bought a small copper jug that
kept refilling with water every time it was emptied. He bought a
cane that turned into a rainbow silk. He bought a device that en-
abled anything he stuffed into his hand to vanish. Then he out-
grew Humpty Dumpty's and moved on to Max Holden's.

Max's was a real *magician's* store. No whoopee cushions or
hand buzzers. It was real, and it bore the posters of legends on
its walls. There were glass cases filled with spring flowers, col-
lapsible doves, huge silks. There were swords and saws and
boxes painted red and black, gold and silver. Magicians came
and bought tricks. They talked about shows: "When I was at
the Albee in Baltimore," they would say, or "I did this club in
Indianapolis." And they would mention names like Scarne and

Peck found himself fiddling with a trick called the "ghost hand-kerchief" while his father talked to Mrs. Giarnarni and read her chart. Mrs. Giarnarni was old. She had hair the color of aluminum siding and lay in a raised bed with bottles hung over her and tubes running from the bottles to different parts of her body. Her face looked like it was crusted. She spoke in a slow and scratchy way. Peck's father said Mrs. Giarnarni owned the best Italian restaurant in North Boston.

"... Dr Peck?" Mrs. Giarnarni asked ... barely.

"Yes, Mrs. Giarnarni," Peck's father, the doctor, said.

"What is that your son's doing?" she asked.

Peck's father turned to see Peck behind him, keeping busy with his ghost. "Oh, my goodness!" Peck's father said and laughed. "Oh, my goodness, look at that! My son's a *magician*," he said to Mrs. Giarnarni. "He loves magic. He does trick after trick. Sometimes we feel it would be better if he did his school work."

Peck was making the ghost dance in mid-air. He felt strange —funny—and put on the spot.

"I started him," his father said, and it seemed to Peck he said it proudly.

Peck felt strange in a *new* way.

"Son? ..." Mrs. Giarnarni said to Peck in her voice that crawled like a bug.

"Yes, ma'am?" Peck said, stuffing the ghost into his pocket.

"Come here. Come ... by me," she said.

Peck's father motioned. Peck drew near.

"Do your trick," Mrs. Giarnarni asked. "Do your trick and make me better."

Peck looked at his father. His father seemed to be shuffling papers inside his head, behind his eyes. He nodded.

"Do your trick and make Mrs. Giarnarni better," he winked.

Peck drew the ghost out of his pocket and began. He told the story about how all the other ghosts laughed at this one because it was so small and couldn't scare anybody and how the ghost had said he didn't want to scare anybody anyway, he just wanted to make people laugh. It was the patter story that had come printed with the trick.

Mrs. Giarnarni listened. She watched and smiled.

Peck's father stood by, a little behind Peck, also smiling.

Peck made the ghost rise. He made it move from side to side. He made the ghost rise up over his shoulder, which was an added twist he himself had invented. Finally, he made the ghost do a somersault in the air.

Mrs. Giarnarni made a sound of pleasure. "If I could clap, I'd clap," she said.

Peck's father said: "That's very good. I don't know I've seen that one. How do you do it?"

"I can't tell," Peck said. A magician didn't tell his tricks, that was the law. That was the credo. He'd heard it over and over at Max Holden's. Some of the older men now were taking Peck under their wing and offering professional confidences. Magicians could only tell secrets to other magicians.

Mrs. Giarnarni laughed. "I feel better already, Doctor," she said.

Peck felt amazing. He felt powerful. In the car on the way home from the hospital, Peck's father again asked the secret to Peck's trick and Peck again refused. The moment after was unspoken but tense. Peck had never defied his father before in that way or felt he knew something his father didn't. It was as if he held some fleeting, subtle power over his father, and it felt strange.

A month later, during their hospital Sunday, Peck asked where Mrs. Giarnarni was.

"She took an amazing turn," Peck's father said. Her blood count went down. Her lungs cleared. She's back running the restaurant."

Peck felt good. It made him feel absolutely powerful. Maybe it was because he had done the ghost for Mrs. Giarnarni that she had gotten better. He asked his father for an expensive gift for his thirteenth birthday two weeks away: a black, red, and gold Mandarin Chinese box, large enough for the appearing or disappearing of a cat or small dog.

"Do you think it's possible you're getting a little carried away," Peck's father said, "with this magic?"

With the parties—the ones Peck found himself newly invited to—there were older high school girls, sometimes a year or two past Peck. Some of them he knew and some he had only seen. Some had smiled at him in the corridors. At one party, after making everybody laugh with a fifteen-minute comedian's patter-book monologue about growing up fat, which was all the funnier because Peck was lank and bony, he amazed the room by producing blazes of fire at his fingertips. There were ooos and ahhs, and when the music was turned back up and the lights further down, two girls came up to Peck at the same time and asked if he would dance.

He knew one of the girls. She was Libby Abbott, someone whose teeth were so white they seemed, even to Peck, to be artificial like a prop. She was a year older, but she had been in an art class with Peck. She had been nice before with greetings and smiles. The other girl's name was Marcia Wolfenstein and she was in the *ninth* grade. Her body rose and fell; it curved in and out like a woman's, and Peck had never seen her until that very night. He said *yes* to Marcia and *maybe later* to Libby Abbott. Peck had never learned to dance, but Marcia obviously knew.

So he fit and moved accordingly and everything seemed to be working out. Marcia moved Peck more than Peck moved her, and before he understood, they were through a door and in an unlit laundry room, the door shut behind them.

"Can you do that trick again," Marcia asked. She was very close.

Peck had one more piece of flash paper and one more match head. He'd glued abrasive on his palm. Diverting Marcia briefly, he got the match head under his fingernail, the flash paper into his palm and ... *Poof! Presto!* ...fire in the dark!

"Jesus Christ!" Marcia said, "is that amazing or what?" And then she said, "Now I'm going to show *you* a trick," and she took Peck's hand and drew it under her sweater. Peck's breath jumped inside him. It seemed almost to leave his throat dry. Then Marcia's mouth was on Peck's mouth, open and wet, her tongue digging entry then finding the insides of his cheeks, the roof of his mouth. Peck felt like a piece of his own flash paper. Then Marcia was apart again, leading him back through the laundry room door and into the dancing party. "You show me your tricks," she said to Peck, "I'll show you mine."

A habit Peck developed to the point of ritual was putting his magic away in the steamer trunk his mother had loaned him. He could not remember ever having been so neat and orderly. He set trick after trick inside the trunk into what he felt should be its proper place. The priority places for the best tricks were angled along the edges and in the corners where the trunk shaped its own enclosure. Sometimes when Peck was falling asleep he would sense a *better place* for a given trick and get up, go to the trunk, open it, and make the necessary rearrangement.

The real mystery, the real fascination, came after he had set the tricks inside and closed the trunk. It was what it felt like to have the magic nearby but out of sight. It was what it felt like for Peck to have magic stored in his room. On those occasions when Peck felt confused or hurt, he might simply go to his room, sit on the worn Karistan, and stare hard at the lid of his trunk.

Over time, Peck formed a friendship with Antony Foley, who was older by two years. Antony Foley was interested in magic. Someone had given him tricks—easy stuff in a box, which Antony had never thought interesting until he'd seen Peck. Peck triggered him. Peck triggered Antony Foley's criminal mind, as well, which was clearly ready for whatever magic and whatever prompt would spur him in that direction. Foley came and introduced himself one day in the corridor. "I've got magic at home," he told Peck.

"Great," Peck said. *What did he have?*

"How should I know?" Antony Foley said. "Come home. I'll show it to you. You can see for yourself and tell me if I can make stuff disappear."

"What do you want to disappear?" Peck asked.

"I dunno. Candy. Baseballs. Cigarettes."

Peck checked out Antony Foley's tricks. They lay strewn in a lidless cardboard box in a corner of the bedroom against Antony's water stained, statue-of-liberty wallpaper. The tricks weren't much. Peck knew them all. Still, he began instruction.

"No disappearing?" Antony said.

No disappearing.

"Never mind then," Antony said and showed Peck his stash of nude polaroids. They were girls from Rye Beach, New Hampshire, where Antony's family had a summer cottage. "Where can I get a disappearing trick?" Antony asked.

Peck marked the appropriate page and brought his catalogue to school, and the next Saturday he took Antony on the MTA subway to Tremont Street and Max Holden's, where they rode the elevator up to the third floor. They walked down the dim hall that crossed over into the world of legerdemain and performance.

"Holy shit! This is amazing!" Antony Foley said.

Peck had the clerk vanish a silk for Antony. They could buy the trick for three dollars. Antony wanted two.

"All you need is one," Peck told him.

"Hey, if something is good, you *never* just need one," Antony said.

He had the clerk teach him the trick. It was standard magician's paraphernalia—an aluminum egg on an elastic, painted flat black with one end of the egg sliced off. You wore a coat, pinned one end of the elastic way up inside your sleeve, palmed the black egg, stuffed the silk into your fist, opened your hand, and extending your arms, *zipp!* ... the elastic retracted the egg-shaped cupful of handkerchief.

"Fabulous!" Antony said. "Fabulous!" It didn't sound, Peck thought, like a word kids used. "I want another one," Antony said, "for my friend here."

Peck protested, but Antony wouldn't listen. Antony pinned both his eggs in place inside his raincoat and had Peck position his egg. "Okay," he said as they left Max Holden's and stepped into the elevator: "Let's rehearse!" Antony hung a right into the first department store. It was called Town & Country.

"But this is a *lady's* store," Peck objected.

Antony raised his eyebrows. "Silk handkerchiefs!" he said.

He led Peck to the handkerchief counter and began to rummage. Peck imitated. He saw Antony stuffing silks into his hand, then lift both hands over his head, fingers spread. "Mama mia!" he exclaimed theatrically: "They got nothin' here! Nothin'! My sister's gonna go nutso!"

"Mama mia!" Peck aped Antony. He was almost laughing. He threw his hands high over his head and could feel the metal egg on the elastic snap up his sleeve.

"Would you boys please put those silk handkerchiefs back?" A salesgirl, who had been standing near and attending, approached the boys.

"What're you talking about?" Antony said.

"Hold your hands out," the woman instructed. Both boys complied. The salesgirl looked mystified. "I saw you stuffing handkerchiefs into your hands," she said.

Peck felt terrified. His father talked all the time, it seemed (when he talked), about right and wrong. His mother always broke into tears when Peck had done something he shouldn't.

"I was just going through them," Antony said. "I was just going through—looking for a red and green one for my sister."

The salesgirl requested that they roll up their sleeves. Peck caught an image of himself in jail.

Antony started rolling and Peck copied him. Both rolled their coat sleeves fold by fold to their elbows. Peck could feel the black metal egg under his armpit, six or seven inches away. But in the stretch running elbow to fingertip, there was only skin.

"I'm sorry," the salesgirl apologized. "I shouldn't have accused you unfairly."

Right or wrong, fair or unfair, this was a new world! Peck imagined sawing the salesgirl in half. He imagined touching her breasts and having each turn into a half-dozen roses. Tomorrow he would eat fire. Tomorrow he would peel the moon like a blood orange. Tomorrow he would open his lunch bag at school and a thousand blue butterflies would rise up.

With the right words, with the right gestures, there was nothing in the world that could not be brought close and made wondrous, moved from light to dark and back again in a single stroke. There was no ghost, it seemed to Peck, that he could not make dance.

t was amazing the windows into a life that magic opened, the unimagined powers inside Peck that he felt through magic. He'd been a baby, barely able to walk and talk inside his own house. Then suddenly, even though the seasons had scarcely changed, he felt like a man! He could say things. Girls approached him. He felt articulate, sexual, and sometimes dangerously criminal.

One day, a song, "Garden in the Rain," came from somebody's radio and Peck sang along. A stranger told him he had a wonderful voice. It was news to Peck; still, he tried out for Glee Club the next day and got a solo. He earned money. He could ride into Boston, walk around the streets like he worked there, go into a hotel or restaurant, order a meal. He could lie. It wasn't hard to make up just anything you felt like saying. It was all just like patter—like the stuff in the magicians' and comedians' joke books. In fact, the more stuff you just made up, the more people seemed to like you, the older you seemed to be, the more power you seemed to have. Peck could skip school and write excuses from his parents. He could commit crimes because, for him, crimes were invisible.

Before, life had always seemed bad—frightening—like something you had to beg to be let in on. Now everywhere he turned, it seemed, life and all the people in life begged for his next joke or his next trick. One day he sat down at his family's Chickering, thought of a song he'd been hearing on the radio, and *played* it. The keys he hit trilled and snapped under his fingers and were mostly right. His mother came in from the kitchen where she was making meatloaf and stood in the archway amazed, listening. "You must have an ear," she said. "I've heard some people have a natural ear ... for music ... and you must have one."

"Just one?" Peck asked.

She laughed. Her laugh was as sweet and fragile as a fall leaf.

Peck loved her laugh. Better, he thought, that she should laugh than cry. Still, he didn't understand his own joke.

For a while, starting when he was about fourteen, he did shows for free at school in all the home rooms that asked him to. He did them during open period. At first it made sense. It was good to practice—and in two months, he was famous. He couldn't go from, say, ancient history to music without thirty people calling Peck! ... Peck!

He began noticing the way people greeted each other. On Sundays at the hospital with his father, he watched how the doctors said hello to their patients, what they did with their mouths, how they stood, if they did anything special with their hands. Different gestures, different smiles. Peck imitated them. He watched when the news reporters on television came on. How *they* held themselves. What kinds of clothes they wore. How *they* smiled. He watched the Celtics being introduced. What were *they* doing to get the crowd so worked up? If there was a parade, he'd skip school and go watch how the people on the floats waved to the crowds. He grew fascinated with the whole notion of celebrity. One time, introduced at a dinner party his parents were having, someone asked: "So, Peck, tell us. What do you want to be when you grow up?"

"A celebrity," Peck said.

"But Peck," his mother observed, "you're barely fifteen." What was her point? he wondered. What did age have to do with it? What did age have to do with anything?

He experimented. His effects grew. He had a repertoire of nearly four dozen tricks from basic sleight of hand to small illusions. He tried to think of ways to mix magic with the piano. He subscribed to a comedian's newsletter. He experimented with singing certain of his patter as if it were light opera. He read every book on the life of Houdini. He grew curious about Uri Geller.

In the middle of a week, Peck's father announced at dinner that the Cleary sisters, long-time patients and important links in Cambridge social circles, had invited the Peck family for tea at their apartment on Memorial Drive. "It seems I've bragged so much about my son, the magician," he said, "that the Clearys want him to perform for them." It seemed a foregone conclusion that Peck would agree to this. Most of what Peck's father said sounded like a conclusion. "And so we'll all be going to the Cleary sisters on Sunday for a brief," he emphasized the word, "*brief* magic show."

Peck resented the assumption that he would perform. He was charging for his performances now. He and Antony Foley had done two children's birthday parties for fifteen dollars apiece, and there were three other *bookings* (Peck had learned the word somewhere) waiting in the wings.

But that Sunday, because he knew that these days, in his

parents eyes, too often he was not dutiful, he hauled seven tricks along to the Cleary sisters. He hated tea. They had no Coke or Seven-up. Their cookies broke the minute you touched them and then they seemed irritated if you got crumbs on something they called their *Tabriz*.

So, when Peck's moment came, he got up somewhat sourly, feeling like a family pet asked to tap the answer to "How much is two plus two." He did his tricks—crowd-pleasers, all of them; all sure-fire—but threaded into his talk a different patter than usual, mostly excerpted from the most recent *Comedian's Newsletter*. He didn't fully understand the meaning of the comic routines, and although he sensed that there might very well be something not quite right with the words *diaphragm* and *french tickler,* he charged on ahead, completing his flourishes in the gathering and frosty silence.

"You humiliated me," Peck's father said in the car driving home.

Peck pled ignorance.

Peck's mother forgave. "Sweetie," she said quietly, cautiously to her husband, the doctor, "Sweetie, he didn't know what he was saying." In the silence, she looked from Peck's father to Peck, Peck to his father.

Peck's father snorted and firmly growled his imperative that this was it, "the end of this entertainment business."

Peck surprised himself with the surety and confidence of his own response. "No," he said, "wrong."

In school, another time, just before he had given up his free performing all together, Peck tried a routine he decided to announce as *hypnotism*. In fact, it was just a practical joke dressed in a mystical motley. And Conley Pfeiffer was to be the butt of it.

Conley Pfeiffer was who Peck would have wanted to be had

he not been drawn to magic. Conley's father was an MIT physicist who shared the Nobel Prize with an Italian two years before. Conley was very smart, although he didn't seem to know what use "smarts" were at the age of fifteen. His skin was almost white. He rarely spoke. And he looked like his bones hadn't gotten hard yet.

It was the home-room open period, as it always was when Peck performed, and Peck selected Conley to be hypnotized. The way it would work, Peck instructed, was that they would sit on chairs facing one another. They were never to break eye contact. Both were to hold china dinner plates against their chests with their left hands. Conley was to mirror Peck's movements with his free right hand. They set up. What Conley couldn't see, but which the rest of the students could see, was that his plate had been coated with candleblack on its backside. Peck filled his voice with incantatory rhythms and started moving his free hand round and round the backside of his clear plate, then swept it across his brow and down his nose and across his cheeks, all the while making more sleepy and haunting rhythms with his words.

Conley followed. He circled his plate. He took his hand away. He swept his sooted fingers across his face, never breaking the instructed eye contact. There were giggles in the room that may have confused him, but he was obedient and shut them out.

"You are getting sleepy," Peck intoned. "It is very hard to keep your eyes open."

Indeed, as all watched Conley, it seemed true.

"You will leave this room. You will go to lunch. You will sit at your lunch table ... and fall asleep into your food," Peck instructed.

Conley was rocking back and forth unstably in his chair.

"Count backwards with me from ten," Peck built toward a

finale. The entire class, including dozy Mr. Morse, their teacher, had hands clamped over their collective mouths to hold the laughter in because Conley looked like an Aborigine with tribal smears everywhere. But there was a kind of wonder, as well, that kept their silence—a wonder which almost fearfully acknowledged that, for all the joke, Conley was clearly entering Peck's hypnotic suggestion.

The show ended and everyone applauded. Some cheered. Peck always loved that. Then the students, including Conley in a kind of weave, wandered off to lunch. Ten minutes later, Conley collapsed face down into his creamed chicken. He was pointed out to Peck two tables away. "Holy shit!" Peck muttered to himself.

Three teachers, the principal, and the vice-principal converged. They were, word for word, a chorus. "Get him out of it," they pleaded. All five were panicked, Peck could see. All five were without means and without resources. Peck studied their eyes. He studied the skin, loose and pale, bereft of muscle tone, on their faces. They were begging. Clearly he was their lone chance. He, Peck, was the sole hope any of them had to bring the son of a Nobel Prize laureate back from some realm of enchantment.

Peck nodded. He stood, and the entire lunchroom fixed their eyes on him. He walked straight over to Conley Pfeiffer's table, stood behind him, placed his hands on Conley's shoulders, and announced in the fullest and most resonant voice he had ever summoned: "Conley ... listen. Listen to me. Listen carefully. ... I will count backwards from ten to zero. When I reach zero, I will clap my hands once ... twice ... three times. On the third clap, you will be awake again."

Then Peck rehearsed precisely what he had described: "Four ... three ... two ... one ... zero!" He clapped. Conley rose, slowly at first, then with clarity and possession, getting up from his creamed chicken, his mask of candleblack still showing through.

That night, lying in bed, moonlight seeping through his dormer window, Peck wondered whether there were any powers in the world which he might not, now or someday, command. He thought about Antony Foley. It intrigued him, the differences between his and Antony's families. Peck had never been in a house like Antony's, whose father was either always there or gone. "What does your father do?" Peck asked Antony. "He closes deals," Antony had said. That night at dinner, Peck asked his parents, "What does it mean to close deals?" and they laughed.

When Antony's father was there, he and Antony's mother seemed to be either fighting or having a party. When they had a party, they drank. Sometimes they drank just with each other, and sometimes there were other people who came by. Antony's mother wore T-shirts all the time—some fancy, some plain. She would always say, "Antony—where are your manners? Offer your friend a drink," when there was a party going on. She wore a lot of make-up. It seemed to Peck it must feel to her that her face weighed a lot, given how much makeup she wore. Peck's mother sometimes wore rouge and sometimes wore a little lipstick, but she never made her eyelids purple and green; she never made her mouth look twice as big as it was.

Antony's parents swore. They swore more when they were fighting, but they swore at their parties, too. And if there were friends partying with them, their friends swore. Once, a redheaded woman named Lisette lifted up her leather skirt and yelled Fuck me! and everyone laughed. The worst Peck had ever heard in his own home was his father when he couldn't find a tool he needed say something like "dammit to hell!"

Antony's mother took a lot of pills when Antony's father wasn't around. She seemed to like to vacuum at such times. Their party friends would come over even when Antony's father was away closing a deal someplace. It seemed to Peck that there was a lot of screaming and laughing going on at Antony's house. Another thing Antony's mother liked to do was throw dishes against the wall when she was unhappy. Peck sometimes crunched pieces of china under his shoes when he walked through their kitchen. He couldn't remember ever seeing his mother throw anything.

Antony's father always had a big wad of hundred-dollar bills in a money clip. He brought the money clip out of his pocket a lot and turn it over and over in his hands, then he'd slip it back. It was like he was trying to remember what to spend his money on. Peck's father carried money because he *bought* things, although Peck had never seen the money.

Antony Foley had a younger sister, Teresa, who was twelve. Everyone in the family was always calling her a *slut*. "Teresa: you're such a slut," Antony's mother would say and laugh. "Where's your slutty sister?" Antony's father would ask. When she would get snoopy and want to see a new trick or hang around to see Antony's polaroids, he would tell her, "Slut brats not allowed." Antony told Peck, "She started getting her period when she was about, like, *seven*."

Peck's younger brother, Nick, got good grades in school and never seemed to do anything wrong. What *was* it between Peck's and Antony's families? What was the difference? How would you say it if you had to? Peck's family was almost invisible, *but it was hard not to pay attention to Antony's family.*

Peck and Antony started making more and more money

with their magic shows. They hired themselves out for children's birthday parties as "Two Guys Who Do Magic." They ran their ad every Friday in *The Citizen*. Peck did most of the show. Antony had four tricks he liked to do. They split the money. Peck believed Antony had gotten into magic because it gave him new and better ways to steal things. In fact, Antony was always scheming and telling Peck how he might use a trick to commit a crime, and Antony's adaptations mostly involved theft; a number of them involved ways to, as Antony put it, "cop a feel." Once, in a convenience store, Antony prompted Peck to astonish the clerk with sleight of hand—spring flowers and silver dollars. Outside in the parking lot, Antony handed Peck three hundred dollars, half of what he had withdrawn from the till. The next day, Peck returned the full amount, making up Antony's half which Antony refused to turn over, out of his own savings. "Hocus-pocus," Peck told the clerk. She broke into tears and thanked him.

Peck thought it was perhaps time to rethink his friendship with Antony. He told him he was going "solo" on the magic act. If Antony wanted to develop an act of his own, Peck would be happy to help him with it. Antony was less than pleased. He responded by bloodying Peck's nose and kicking him in the groin. He said: "Hey—and that's just the start of it. I'm getting revenge!" It seemed their friendship was over.

Perhaps understandably, Peck's business boomed without Antony Foley's partnership. He could do six magic shows a week in his own and surrounding towns. He had a motor scooter that had a sidecar for his paraphernalia trailer, an arrangement which was both unstable and cumbersome. One time when his motor scooter toppled over, Peck had to give his show with blood seeping into his eyes from his gashed forehead. The family thought it was make-up, thought it was all intended as a spook-house routine.

By the time he turned sixteen, Peck had twelve thousand dollars in the bank. The day after he secured his driving license, he returned home with a new Subaru Justy. "That's a nicer car than mine!" Peck's father said. And then Dr. Peck said: "So, what are we going to do about your grades?"

Grades seemed a strange word to Peck. It sounded unnecessary and indecipherable—like one of the words his father sometimes explained as *Yiddish*. What did grades have to do with anything, especially for a person who had just paid twelve thousand cash for a new Subaru.

It was the last time that Peck's father, the doctor, ever raised the subject of school. Something grew in him, something beyond discouraged and closer to defeated. After that, for whatever reason, Dr. Peck seemed almost unaware of his son—in a different way than Peck had felt his father remain unengaged in the past. Once, several months later, Peck heard his father say to someone over the phone, "No, my son's not a student."

The week after Peck brought his new Justy home, when he approached it to drive it home from the school parking lot, he saw that someone had carved "REFENGE!!" in nearly foot-high block letters in the paint on the driver's side. Peck knew who it had to be. Only one person he knew spelled that badly, and it was Antony Foley.

REFENGE!! REFENGE!! Who would the police suspect if suddenly Antony Foley vanished? Would Antony's family notice? If they did, might they not applaud? It occurred to Peck for the first time that there were people in the world whose disappearance would be welcome. A great magician could be a kind of mercenary. *Poof!* and no more Antony Foley. *Poof!* and no more Hitler or Joe McCarthy. Peck felt inspired. Holy men were magicians of a sort. Magicians could, in their way, be holy.

About this time, Peck discovered some art skills. One day in Mr. Delorian's class, he'd moved a piece of charcoal around the leaf of a sketch pad and begun scribbling until the image of a shoe appeared. "Talent!" Mr. Delorian had announced. With this new skill, Peck detailed Antony's REFENGE!! on the side of his car into the image of a theater marquee. Classmates rechristened Peck "Broadway." He asked Antony if he wanted a ride. Antony was hesitant.

"Hop in," Peck invited.

Antony slid in cautiously.

Peck started his engine. "I'm going to show you a trick," Peck smiled.

"What're you talking about," Antony asked.

"I'm going to show you how a car goes from zero to a hundred and forty," Peck said.

Antony tried to get out, but Peck had locked the doors.

"Actually, what's going to happen," Peck said, "is that tonight you're going to dream you're in this car and that we're going that fast. You can get out now."

The next day when he found Peck, Antony's face was white. "How'd you do it?" he asked.

Peck smiled.

"I had the dream. The dream you said I'd have. How'd you do it?"

Peck put a hand on Antony's shoulder. "I turned myself into a worm and got inside your brain," Peck said.

"Why?!" Antony's eyes were wide.

"*Refenge,*" Peck said.

The older girls like Marcia Wolfenstein, who had been

Peck's sexual tutors, were graduating from high school and Peck began to notice girls his own age. He decided to date them. Turnabout was fair play. Now it was *his* turn to do the teaching. He'd been grateful, and now others would be. His scheme, if that was the right word to describe it, worked decently until Peck asked out Jessica Entemann.

Jessica was a fan, that was clear. Peck would launch into some routine of legerdemain or comedy and Jessica's eyes would enlarge and beam light, then she'd erupt with laughter. If it wasn't laughter, there would be other sounds of enchantment, of delight—sounds coming from, Peck thought, the back of her neck sometimes, sometimes from her throat. This, of course, occurred in whatever high school classrooms they shared: Mr. Hatch's English, Mme. Lenay's French. They'd never actually gone out. Occasionally, Peck would walk with Jessica to where their homebound journeys diverged. When Jessica asked Peck that December, their senior year, if he would go with her to the girls' choice dance, it seemed right. She was an apt candidate. Who knew what pleasures she and Peck might discover together.

Peck picked her up. Her father was a dentist who wore a bow tie. He looked like he'd been outside shoveling his driveway; his cheeks had that burning winter look. Jessica's mother looked like a mother from some television program where the family is rich and looks down on a lot of people. Peck was polite. He didn't try to make any jokes. Jessica looked nervous. When she introduced them, her voice shook a little. "Clear your throat, Jessie," her mother said.

"Oh, a piano!" Peck said out of nowhere and apropos of nothing. He sat down and banged out a boogie woogie piece. "What's this all about?" he heard Jessica's father, the dentist, asking in the background.

"You look very pretty." Peck began his preparations in the car, driving.

"I'm still amazed you said you'd go with me," Jessica said. "My mother never plays anything but Chopin on that piano." She put a hand in her mouth and bit a fingernail.

Peck reached over and took her hand. She seemed shocked. He kept it, but she tried to pull it away. Peck gave her hand a gentle squeeze and enclosed it. He had produced live white doves at his fingertips, feathers like milkweed fluttering in the air, and he had gone to bed with amazed older girls several times, but he had never held a girl's hand.

At the dance, Jessica nestled so tightly and closely into Peck that he began to sweat. Partly it felt to Peck like she was on some high cliff and almost panicked of loosening her grip. Partly it felt like she'd fallen asleep there. They danced that way all night: slow-dancing to even the frenzied numbers. They said practically nothing. Peck didn't get it. Usually women pulled him this close in exchange for entertainment. He wasn't astonishing her. He wasn't making her laugh. He was just letting her hold onto him and swaying with her on a dance floor. What was the deal?

After the dance, as soon as they were inside his car—the engine on, heater humming—Peck leaned across to Jessica to kiss her. She said no.

"Excuse me?" Peck's response was involuntary.

"No," Jessica said. "No ... please."

"Okay." Peck shifted out of neutral and into first. Again, he didn't get it.

On the way home, they talked. The talk was easy and unblocked now. The awkwardness seemed to have bled out. Jessica seemed glad and not needful or scared anymore. She asked Peck where he was going to college.

25

"I don't know," Peck said. "I may not go. I do okay on tests, but I never do homework, so my grades aren't that good."

"But you're so smart," Jessica said.

Peck pulled a line out of his past. It was one, obviously, he hadn't forgotten. "Maybe I'll just go off and be a celebrity," Peck said.

Jessica's grades, Peck knew, were good. She was planning on going to Berkeley.

When they got back, Jessica had her door open before Peck could turn off the engine. What was with her? He walked her to her door and tried again for a kiss. Again, she said no. It was weird. Here was the first girl who Peck actually wanted to kiss ... just to *kiss*. She had held him on the dance floor as though she would die if she let go. And she was saying no. Peck wondered, if he called out to the University of Colorado where Marcia Wolfenstein was going, if Marcia could explain this to him or if it would be out of even her realm?

What Peck could not know, of course, driving home that night with the solid click of Jessica's front door shutting echo in his brain, was that this was to be their pattern. Over some years, Jessica would confuse him. She would clutch sometimes with what seemed to be an almost brutal neediness, only to abruptly shift and seem unable to set some barrier between them fast enough. And Peck, in turn, according to their pattern, would continue not knowing what to do.

A woman who would *not* confuse Peck was Leslie Fay. She was a mother who hired Peck to do a birthday party for her eight-year-old daughter, then called Peck to return the next day. Whatever Jessica Entemann feared, Leslie Fay *did not*. For every inhibition which Jessica Entemann clung to, Leslie Fay loosed four. Peck had been educated and had learned lessons, but Leslie Fay took him on a post-doctoral whirlwind that left his mind numb. There were afternoons when it felt like Peck's teeth were clamped to his brain. "You are so good for me," Leslie Fay would say, and Peck couldn't imagine how that could be the case.

Leslie Fay introduced Peck to wine. They had wine in bed, wine in her bathtub. Leslie's husband, Michael, traveled. He imported goods. *Wine is nectar,* Leslie Fay would say, and distilled liquor was like stain remover, furniture polish; bourbon and gin were "industrial-strength drinks." Holding her curiously scarred abdomen as if to vomit, she would say, "And *beer!*…"

One afternoon Leslie Fay asked whether Peck had any friends.

"I have *only* friends," Peck said. "Except … I'll tell the truth, one enemy."

"Watch out for the one enemy," Leslie Fay said.

But Leslie was good to him. Even so, Peck got busier and busier with his shows and had little time for her. After a while, he rarely saw her. She said simply, "When you need a break …" She seemed genuinely fond of Peck. She could be as sweet as Peck's own mother when they drank their wine. She would soap his back in the bathtub. That she could make his eyes roll backwards in his head such that, Peck swore, he could see his own skeleton, was a separate matter.

Peck sent Leslie Fay a Piaget watch. It cost him eight hundred dollars. That's how grateful he was. On the card, he wrote: "For a good time …" and hoped she would think it funny. When she ran into him in the village the next week, she objected. "Peck, … you can't give me presents," she said. He of course told her that he could. He had fifteen thousand dollars in the bank, so he could do anything he liked. Even that was a lie. He had over twenty thousand dollars in the bank.

One afternoon in early May, at perhaps his last visit with Leslie and his high school days in their countdown, she said to him in the tub: "Who am I to you?"

What was she asking? Peck's face telegraphed that he held that question.

"Who am I to you?" Leslie Fay repeated. She didn't seem angry or sad or anything. It just seemed a question that was in her head. She reached her finger out from the warm water and traced Peck's lips.

Peck thought. *Who was Leslie Fay to him?*

"Is it hard to say?" she asked. "Is it a hard question?"

"You're amazing—for one thing," Peck said.

"Am I?" Leslie Fay said. "In what way?"

"Nothing ever seems to bother you," Peck observed.

Leslie Fay threw her head back and laughed.

"And you never get tired," Peck said, emboldened. "And you're always inventing new stuff for us to do. I don't know where you get it."

"I don't know where I get it either," Leslie Fay said and smiled. And then she said: "So, is that who I am? Is that it? The unflappable lady? The lady who never gets tired, who keeps inventing stuff? Does that pretty much sum it up for you?

"No, you're *more*," Peck said.

"Tell me."

But Peck couldn't. Some thoughts came, words he thought he might say, but they all seemed to be flooded. They all drowned. And Peck started to cry. Then Leslie Fay started to cry. She came to him a new way, directed, improvised. The water slid back and forth across them, warm, making quiet splashes. "Oh, you dear, dear boy," Leslie kept saying; "Oh, you dear, dear boy." When it was over and they lay in towels, Leslie told Peck who he was to her. She said he was someone who was both young and old, very sure of himself and not at all. "You seem amazed that Creation has given you a life … and at the same time, you act like nothing in that life could ever be impossible." She concluded that he had never once, ever to her, said no.

It was true, Peck had to admit. With Leslie Fay, things mattered in a different way, and it was a world in which you didn't need to say no.

three

F irst of all, Peck had never opened the results of his college aptitude and achievement scores. Second, he had very quickly hidden them when they arrived in the mail that winter from the testing center at Princeton. He had slipped the envelope into a huge old dictionary in the family den. But then, on the same afternoon Peck was taking his last bath with Leslie Fay, Peck's younger brother, Nicholas, found the envelope and, hungry for praise, showed it to Peck's mother, who that evening—feeling herself between two betrayals—showed it to Dr. Peck.

At breakfast, Peck's father made public their discovery. "Do you have any idea what these are?" he asked Peck.

Peck didn't have a trick or escape for this one.

"You're in the ninety-sixth percentile in ability," Peck's father said.

Peck took a deep breath. He picked at his lower lip where it was chapped.

"You know, what I get least," Peck's father went on, "is how you managed to get a 738 in English and a 770 in mathematics."

"Is that bad?" Peck said.

"No," Peck's father said. "It's not bad. That's the point. It's very good."

"Oh," Peck said. And then rising said: "Listen, I'll see you guys later. I need to get to school."

"Have you applied to any colleges?" Dr. Peck shouted from the front door.

"I didn't think I'd get in," Peck called over the engine of his Subaru. He backed out of the driveway. His father seemed frozen in the doorway ... with his mother's head, like a balloon, bobbing over his father's shoulder. Above them, Peck could see Nick's face—white and achingly uncertain—framed in an upstairs window.

It was after the deadline, when college acceptances had already been mailed, that Peck even applied, but he still managed to get into Colby College in Maine, the University of Massachusetts, and Bard College in upper New York state. He chose Bard. "I think the other two have more structure," his father tried to advise, which made Peck feel that if such a choice could be right, he had made it. His father gave him a reading list, which he tore up. His mother produced luggage catalogs and asked Peck if he saw anything he liked.

"I keep looking for something I can do for you," his mother said.

"You already do. You do it every day," Peck said.

His mother looked sad, happy, confused.

Peck spent the summer doing shows. His reputation had spread. Families from his home town vacationed up and down the coast, so one day he might drive up to the Magnolia Country Club in Essex to do magic, another day he might drive down to Marion near the Cape to use his comedy and emcee a dance at the yacht club. He was up to seventy dollars a job now. His bank account scared him. What could he do with that amount of money? He offered to pay for his education, but his father said, "Don't insult me." In the hours when Peck wasn't performing, he would usually do one of three things. He would go out to the beach or to the pool by, say, the yacht club and swim and tan. Or he would go to the movies and watch the way the stars acted certain emotions. His favorites were Paul Newman, Steve Martin, and Martin Sheen. There was a revived burlesque house in Boston near Chinatown where Peck went even though the dancers mostly made him feel sick. The comedians were good. And there were interesting ideas for acts, even when the people didn't have very much talent. Peck got the idea at the burlesque house that he should learn to juggle, that it probably wasn't all that hard, that there were certain objects that were easy but *looked* difficult.

One day, Peck got the idea of getting on a plane and flying to New York where a magician he admired, Hopewell, was playing. Hopewell did an entire act with large tropical fish and parrots. The whole stage was dressed to look like some Polynesian island. Ultraviolet fish appeared stunningly in absolutely empty 200-gallon aquariums. Parrots materialized on the fronds of coconut palms. Then Hopewell would snatch the parrots by their rubbery legs and hurl them up and into the air above his head where they would disappear in a flash of fire. You could hear the audience gasp. People loved having the impossible happen and being on hand when it happened.

One Monday morning at breakfast, Peck told the others of his family that he would see them on Friday.

"Do you mean *tonight?*" his mother asked.

Peck said, "No, Friday."

Dr. Peck asked where his son thought he was going. Did he

have a magic show in Hyannis Port or somewhere?

Peck said no, that he was flying to Las Vegas. Mainly it was because there were two magicians at a casino there who performed with wild animals: anacondas and panthers. "I need to see someone vanish a panther," Peck said.

Peck's father said that would be absolutely impossible.

"So it seems," Peck said.

Dr. Peck said no, that wasn't the point he was making. How did Peck think he was going to get to Las Vegas?

"Obviously, on an airplane," Peck said.

Peck's father said no.

Peck said yes.

There was a silence.

"That's four days from now," Peck's mother said.

"And where do you think you'll stay there?" Peck's father asked.

Peck had made reservations, he said. "I'm seventeen years old. I have twenty-two thousand dollars in the bank. If I want to go to Las Vegas, I'll go to Las Vegas."

Peck's mother asked that her husband, Dr. Peck, try to be understanding. "We're lucky he has such a gift," she said.

"The gift of a low-life," Dr. Peck grumbled.

Peck's mother said she hoped Dr. Peck wasn't going to put his foot down. "Trust him," she said.

"I don't know why," Peck's father said to his son, "you want to go to a place like that. I don't know why you have this fascination with riff-raff."

"What's a riff-raff?" Peck's younger brother, Nick, asked.

"A riff-raff is what your brother seems intent to become," Peck's father said.

"Dear, don't say something you'll regret later," Peck's mother inserted.

Peck observed the way her open hands pressed against her chest.

Peck flew to Las Vegas. The two magicians were good, but that wasn't the point. They were doing basic magic, basic illusion. They just blew everything up. What Peck did with gerbils and doves, they did with panthers and anacondas. The point wasn't that they were skillful. The point was that they dared to do it. And the point was that as far as the audience was concerned, they couldn't dare enough. Peck learned something from that.

He also went to see two separate, very-much-older-but-fabled comedians stand essentially alone on stage, each for an hour and a half, and hold showrooms overflowing with gamblers in the palms of their hands. Peck learned something there, too. He learned it was less the joke than the style. It was less the wit than the presence. There were people who could walk on a stage and, before they even uttered a syllable, have everyone in the auditorium percolating with laughter.

Also that summer, halfway through August, Peck tried again with Jessica Entemann. It was their fourth date. Peck knew in a matter of weeks they would be heading off to different campuses. He tried something different. He rented a limousine and a chauffeur for two hundred dollars and arrived at her door in a cutaway tuxedo. They were going to a movie, *Three Coins in the Fountain.* The expression on Jessica's face when she opened her door communicated to Peck that this would be all wrong. "Oh, Peck!" she said, and sighed. He said he'd be back in a half hour.

A half hour later, he arrived in soft Levi's and a casual jacket.

"Have we missed the movie?" Jessica Entemann asked.

"We'll think of something," Peck said. He got on the highway.

"Where are we going?"

"Toward New Hampshire," Peck said.

"For what?" Jessica asked.

"Variety," he answered. And then he asked: "What's the deal with us?"

"What's what deal with us?" Jessica asked.

"I get confused when I'm with you," Peck said.

"I get confused when I'm with *you*," Jessica said.

"Okay," Peck said. "So, ... what? We have a relationship based on confusion?"

"I guess," Jessica said.

"Who am I to you?" Peck said, remembering Leslie Fay's question.

"*What?*" Jessica asked.

"Who am I to you?" he repeated, thinking Leslie Fay knew her stuff. This was an effective gambit.

"I don't know," Jessica said. "Sometimes I wonder that myself. I guess the thing is, ..." She considered for a moment. "The thing is ... that nothing seems to stop you."

"Right," Peck said. "Except you."

"Excuse me?"

"I said right, except you. ... Never mind." Then he did a crossover, swung the car south again, and headed home.

"Why did you even ask me out in the first place?" Jessica asked.

"Hey, you asked me first," Peck said.

"Oh, ... that's right," Jessica said. "You didn't want to?"

"That's not the point," Peck said.

"What's the point?" Jessica asked.

"I don't know," Peck said. "I guess I'd like you to fall madly in love with me."

"I *am* madly in love with you," Jessica said.

Peck scrambled for words. "You pick up a sledgehammer every time I try to kiss you," he said.

"I'm afraid if I let you, it will all be over," Jessica said.

"*What* will be over?"

"I don't know," she said. "Just whatever."

They pulled up in front of Jessica's house.

"So is this our date?" she asked. "Eleven o'clock? This is it? It's over?"

"I guess so," Peck said. He was mad, though he had no real sense for what he was mad about.

"You're not a virgin, are you?" Jessica Entemann said.

Peck found himself breathing hard. It was the heavy breath of an anger and not of passion. "You're babbling," he said. "You're just babbling stuff. I don't understand it."

So Jessica Entemann threw open her door and ran up her walk and flew into her house. Peck watched the lights go off inside. Then he saw faces in the dark: first the dentist father's, then the proper mother's, then Jessica's itself, pressed, cloaked by darkness, against three different windows.

Peck drove off. He sensed that this was one of many moments, many nights like this, to come. He understood in some curious way that his and Jessica's lives, whatever they would be, would stretch into their future.

Peck's college career was short-lived. He drove himself to Annandale-on-the-Hudson in his Subaru, Antony Foley's RE-FENGE still in Broadway-lit lettering on the car's side. His mother cried when he carried his suitcases down the stairs. His father stood in the driveway with him for half an hour, giving advice, speaking about how life can change and about "transition points." The family dog, Aesculapius (Scap for short), barked and barked as though Peck were an intruding delivery man. Peck's brother, Nick, shot baskets the whole time.

Peck took the long route through New York City, staying over night before continuing up the Hudson along the expressway to Annandale. In the city, he ate dinner at Sardi's. He had made a reservation. That much he knew about eating in the city. Still, the *maître de* seemed annoyed to seat only him. "Will your parents be joining you?" he asked. Peck tipped the *maître de* and ordered veal oscar and Pouilly Fuisse by the glass. He had cappuccino at the meal's end and a glass of cognac. Peck was eighteen years old. He had enough money in the bank to put a down payment on a house. He was going off to be … what? A freshman in college. In the dining room were actors he recognized—comedians, celebrities. What was he going to be spending his time doing? Writing compositions? It seemed as though his life were moving backwards.

He went to a Broadway show that night. It was a musical. He had read in *Variety* that the days of Broadway musical comedy were numbered, perhaps soon a thing of the past. It didn't seem so, and Peck found that he loved the extravagance. He loved the flourishes and flash, the brash, unapologetic style. A legendary comic once said that the recipe for the stage was an ounce of talent, five gallons of style, and to mix vigorously. Peck walked out of the theater singing the reprieved song and doing a little dance. Halfway down the block on 46th Street, a man in a Chesterfield coat, passing, handed him five dollars. Peck took a cab downtown to Village Gate, where he watched four extremely clever and inventive, very funny young performers in a review. Watching, he felt his whole chest cavity tighten. He felt it thicken and grow hard at the thought that in the morning he had to drive off to four years of classrooms and hour-long exams and term papers. In his bed that night at the Americana, he found himself in tears.

Bard College was a pleasant surprise. He had never visited and was somewhat relieved by what he encountered. It was the day before classes would start, and the college president talked to all the incoming freshmen. "This should be the most explorative and creative period of your lives," he told them: "There should be no limits, no boundaries or limits or barriers!" Peck left the lecture feeling a new buoyancy. The college's charismatic president set a fire in Peck that burned brightly for a week. Peck wrote poems and read them nights in the college coffee shop. He stretched a canvas and painted a white dove, in oils, rising above a magician's fingertips. He created a comedy routine using six-pack and twelve-pack cardboard beer containers. He wrote a cabaret review of what he had seen at the Village Gate, which had fired him into invention. He paired up with a young man from New York to sing doo-wah rock-and-roll numbers. He couldn't, of course, pull himself away from magic. He'd brought two trunks of tricks. He did some juggling. He did some hypnotism and ventriloquism. He tried out for the college's first dramatic production, a play by someone named Maeterlinck, which he didn't understand. He got the lead.

But by the second week, Peck could feel the tension between what he wanted to do and what his schedule and courses told him he was supposed to do. "Did you do your trig?" someone would say, and his brain would feel clamped, his eyes would burn.

So as things ended up, Bard College did not become an extended experience. In a single September, he had caught the fire lit by the president's speech and felt it just as quickly die out.

In October he went into a depression. He only went to half of his classes, otherwise wandering endless hours along the Hudson and exploding in and out of an affair with a girl from Carbondale, Illinois, named Patricia Flint. The night after they'd met, Patricia said she was pregnant, then the next week attempted suicide because, she said, she had aborted the child. Student health took her in. She got sent home. After Patricia's departure, Peck stayed in his room listening to Hindemith and Charlie Parker and set fire to two of his favorite magic illusions.

In November he made some friends. All of them, like Peck, were dissatisfied with the college and felt that its president, in his opening remarks, had lied to them. Peck and his friends, whose names were Amy, Russell, and Fernando, created an alternative student newspaper. They also shot a ten-minute half-pornographic, half-surrealist film based, as Fernando said, on the life and works of Charlie Chaplin. They demonstrated against a bank in nearby Red Hook for not employing Native American tellers. Also in November, Peck developed a new music-and-magic routine: in the midst of playing a medley of songs, all with garden and flower references in their titles, he produced endless leaves and blooms from the open lid of a Yamaha piano. The piano sprouted bouquets of roses, fat-headed hydrangea, succulent and ivy plants, and potted poinsettia.

The activities of November spilled somewhat over into December when Peck went home, mid-month, for vacation. Peck's father seemed to be waiting for him in the garage. "I was just putting away the snow blower," he said. "How's it gone? You haven't set records, exactly, for correspondence."

"I'm meeting a lot of people," Peck said.

"What about your courses?"

"What about my courses?" Peck asked.

"Are you managing to keep your nose to the grindstone?" Dr. Peck wondered.

"I'm not sure—maybe—whatever it might mean," Peck said.

Peck's mother cried on seeing him again. Scap, the dog, barked. Nick, Peck's younger brother, said: "What's it like?"

"It's sort of like Cub Scouts," Peck replied.

"Lanyards, you mean? Pine car derbies?"

"Like that, yeah," Peck said, "only bigger." Peck hooked his brother's head into the crook of his elbow, squeezed, and knuckled his hair. Something about Nick's eyes, about his unsure and too-loud voice, made Peck sad.

Peck tried passing his holidays without incident, cooperatively, but felt like he was in a foreign country. His room, with its faded wallpaper, seemed like the room of some other person: a visitor, guest, someone who he'd only heard about but never met. He stared at what, until now in his life, he had hung on the walls and wondered every day whose stuff it was. He bought his family presents but had no sense of who he was buying them for. When asked about himself and Christmas, what he wanted, he had no notion of what to say. He called Jessica Entemann.

"Why are you calling me?" she asked.

"How's Berkeley?" Peck said.

"It's wonderful. I love it. I'm doing well in my classes. How's Bard?"

"*Not* wonderful," Peck said and hung up.

Jessica called him back. "Why did you call me?" she asked.

"I can't figure it."

"I can't figure it either," Peck said. "But maybe someday I will.

In January, Bard had what they called their "intersession." It was their scheme for saving money on heating, postponing spring semester a few weeks, but Peck didn't inform his parents, and on the third of the month he just left. He drove to New York City, spent a week, saw shows, went to clubs, looked up his friend Russell who lived on East 87th Street near the park. Peck tried some drugs, but all he did was sneeze for three hours. He flew out to Las Vegas to see a different magician and a different comedian.

From Las Vegas, he flew to Los Angeles. He visited studios, went to the beach, made an appointment with an agent at William Morris, who told him: "Listen, you'd have to live here ... have to take up residency before an agent would even piss on you." Peck ate dinner at a place called Arthur Harry's and saw Danny Kaye eating alone in a corner booth. But then a beautiful black girl joined him.

On about the 27th of January, Peck flew back to New York and drove up to Bard to take his final exams. He got an A on his English exam, flunked chemistry, flunked History of the Renaissance, and got a C in sociology. Someone who identified himself as Peck's advisor called and said Bard was having to put him on something called "equivocal probation." It began to seem like high school all over again except the people were smarter.

February was a strange month. Peck couldn't focus, and not only because it was spring semester. He studied the print on a page ... and it blurred. He looked at a given professor reading a poem by, say, Yeats, and poetic passions aside, the man's face would just melt. Tapes in the college French lab bled ...

word into word. Friends blurred into other friends. Meat blurred into vegetables on his plate in the dining hall. Cars blurred into trucks as Peck watched them across the river on the interstate.

He had the sense that he was at a crisis point. His friend Russell was at the point of crisis, too. Things weren't blurring for him so much as they were being drowned out. He was getting a lot of roaring in his ears. He had them de-waxed and that helped some. But for an entire week, Russell and Peck decided there was no point and just skipped classes and walked endlessly through the snow, through the rain, along the river, up the road, up and down the stairs of their dorm, and discussed whether they should give up college, abandon it and see what other directions and choices might lie ahead. At week's end, one of them decided to leave, the other to stay. Peck re-packed his car and they stood beside it saying their farewells.

"I think you're doing the right thing." Peck said to encourage Russell in his rededication.

"Jesus, I hope so," Russell said. "I'm gonna miss you."

"Hey, out of mind is not out of sight," Peck quipped, "or something like that."

Russell laughed. "I hope we can keep in touch," he said. "I hope we don't just disappear from each other's lives. That would be awful."

Peck felt a shudder. He had told Leslie Fay that all he had were friends, aside from a single enemy, but that had been a lie. He had never had a real comrade in his life, not a comrade like Russell. "You'll hear from me," Peck said. "You'll hear from me. I mean it. That's a promise."

And then Peck did something he'd never done with another male: he took Russell in his arms and embraced him, kissed his friend on the side of his head.

Pulling out of Annandale with the taste of Russell's hair

still in his mouth, Peck repeated his pledge. *You can't just leave people,* he said to himself. *You can't just go away and never appear again.* It seemed important. Something in the idea seemed to be very, very right. *What was he telling himself?* he wondered. *What was he trying to understand?* It seemed, driving his RE-FENGE Subaru in the dark along the Hudson Parkway, he was trying to scream something across a roaring, cresting river ... yell it to a Peck who was all alone on the other bank. He was not sure exactly, on one side, what he was trying to say and, on the far side, what it was he was hearing.

Four

P eck placed no call to his parents. He drove down the Hudson into Manhattan, where he took a room at the Century Paramount Hotel on 47th Street and noticed that everyone in the elevators spoke a foreign language. From the *Manhattan Yellow Pages*, Peck copied the numbers and addresses of thirty agents. Out of the *New York Times* he also copied two dozen apartment listings. Two days later, he was situated in a loft on Pell Street in Chinatown and had been ignored or thrown out of seventeen agents' offices.

He bought some furniture from a store calling itself the Warehouse Giant on Canal Street—a mattress, table, two chairs, a bookcase, lounger, and a twenty-one-inch television. The store said their low prices didn't allow delivery. Peck found a fifteen-year-old black kid named Chad a block away and hired him to help carry—through four trips, eight blocks, five flights of stairs, to his apartment above a tiny restaurant called Wan Nam. "This shit be heavy!" Chad said. Peck gave Chad a hundred dollars and showed him two tricks. "Where dat mu'fugga go?" Chad said, asking after a vanished crystal ball. "Where dat mu'fugga *be* at?"

Chad introduced Peck to two older friends, one from Cuba, one from the West Indies. "Fast hands!" Chad said of Peck to Tyrone and Louis. "This cat do magic!" Tyrone and Louis introduced Peck to something they called "the Monte," and though Peck had never seen it specifically before, he knew the moves. Using the box Peck's television came in, the three began to work. "This be our trav'ling stage," Tyrone said of the box. "*Voila!* The theater of Monte," Louis announced. Soon they were on the street. Louis worked the crowd, Tyrone shilled. Chad kept an eye out for the police. The first day, they pulled down four hundred dollars, which they split three ways. "We take care o' Chad," Tyrone said.

Peck felt bad. That night in his loft, he understood he'd conned decent people out of wages. Sometimes he made wallets disappear in his show for a laugh. Just for the drama, for the anxiety and the suspense. He invariably picked them out of thin air again, usually—in his shows up and down the north and south shores of Massachusetts—with a gift certificate "Dinner for Two at Mama G's" as a bonus. It was something he and Mrs. Giarnarni had worked out. But here, with his new cadre, deception wasn't ultimately a delight. It was a loss; it was a hardship; it was some good citizen's pain. Peck felt he couldn't continue.

The following morning, Peck tried to make his position known. Tyrone and Louis and Chad laughed like tropical birds. *Perhaps,* Peck thought, *English isn't their first language.* Then Chad brought in the stage, and before Peck was able to try to make himself more clear, the crowd was deep and the day's Theater of Monte had begun again. That day, Tyrone divided nearly seven hundred dollars. "We in *show* business!" he said; "We on *tour!*"

What to do, was the question. Antony Foley had carved

REFENGE on the side of Peck's Justy because Peck had dared abandon what Antony obviously considered a two-person Mafia. And that had been in a select Boston suburb. What price would three street-wise New Yorkers exact? Peck had placed himself in a tough position. He didn't even have a woman to comfort him. He had sloughed the promises of higher education. He had betrayed the bonds of friends and family. And now, living above what his father would call an opium den from the sheer pungency, Peck had said "I do" to deception and conspiracy. He turned on his television.

The second show Peck watched featured a detective, and it began to make Peck feel even more guilty. The detective was trying to help a man who had fallen from the back of a pick-up truck and had struck his head. The man had partial amnesia. Some things about his life, the man remembered, some things he didn't. Some things he had always been able to do and could perform by rote. Other tasks, although he had done them nearly all his life, his hands fumbled over. He could cast a fly rod ... but couldn't tie his shoe. He could juggle oranges ... but couldn't play the guitar. Peck went out to an all-night drugstore and bought ten dollars' worth of gauze bandages.

The next morning when the gang of three came to get him, they found Peck with his head thatched with bandages, a wide and ugly blood-dark spot just off-center in the pack. "Wha happen, Bro?" Tyrone asked.

"What? ..." Peck droned in a voice drifting like the scent of ginger up the building stairs.

"Man's head got beat," Chad said.

"What's my name?" Peck asked.

"You Peck," Tyrone said.

"I who?" Peck said.

"You *Peck*."

"*I'm* Peck?"

He explained how he'd had too much to drink and fallen against a fire hydrant. He said he'd found his way home but wasn't sure how he had managed. Pointing to his magic, he asked whether any of them knew what the various objects were for. The three looked at each other.

They took Peck out onto the street and reviewed what they'd been doing. Peck nodded, then wrinkled his brow. He used the sense-memory techniques he'd learned his fall semester in a Bard College acting class.

Louis gathered a crowd and Tyrone shilled; Chad kept the eagle eye. The new day's Monte game began. A man with a beard, wearing a Loden coat, put up twenty dollars. Peck moved the cards. The man guessed the red card against the two black. Peck turned the man's card over … and he was right! Louis and Tyrone looked at each other. Someone in the crowd said "Pay him!" Louis handed over the man's twenty and another twenty. "I got a lock on this," the man said. He was ready for a roll and quickly produced a fifty.

Tyrone and Louis, in the background, made eye contact. The man gave his fifty to Louis to hold. Peck moved the cards. The man guessed, and Peck turned the card. Winner! Louis looked angry. He gave the man two fifties. "That's all we have!" he announced. "We have no more money to play with. This man's eyes too quick!"

"I have money," Peck announced.

"Oh, shit!" he heard Tyrone say in the background.

The crowd was eager and stepped forward to bet with the man. The crowd won. It won again. "Game's over!" Louis announced. He stepped forward and closed it all down. "I don't care if you do still have money," he said to Peck. "Our man is *brain damaged,*" he said to his friends. Louis and Tyrone and

Chad walked off as if Peck were a total stranger. Peck never heard from them or saw any of them again.

Peck saw four more agents, all with the same results. Money wasn't the issue. Peck had transferred his account to a bank called CityFirst and had eighteen thousand still in his account. But what was he going to do with his life?

He tried a new tack. There was an agent named Lefty Swift whose office was in a building on Eighth Avenue between 40th and 41st Streets. It was above a topless bar. Peck made no appointment; he simply went up and sat. There was a small hallway that doubled as an anteroom, without a secretary. It had three cafeteria chairs. Peck sat in the anteroom space for two and a half hours. Lefty's office door was cracked open, so Peck could hear him on the telephone. Lefty's two favorite words were *asshole* and *scumsucker*. At one point, Peck heard Lefty say "Cat act! Cat act!? What sort of asshole wants a scumsucking cat act?" and heard him slam down the telephone. Peck rose from his cafeteria chair and moved to Lefty's office door. He drew it open. He said, "Excuse me, Mr. Swift, sir, but I have a cat act. And I was wondering whether ..."

"Just a minute! Just a minute!" Lefty Swift said to him. "Don't move." He snatched his phone up and began to dial. "I have your cat act," he said to somebody at the other end of the line.

The deal was a week at a hundred dollars a night at a club in Hoboken, New Jersey, and the job started tomorrow. Peck said *fine*. He gave Lefty Swift his name and social security number and left. Two hours later he was in his Justy, heading across the bridge to Hoboken, seven of his best tricks in the back seat.

He found the club. Three blocks away was the Blue Ribbon

Motel. Peck got a room and looked up the closest animal shelter. He adopted three cats and bought a cat carrier. He named the cats Leslie, Russell, and Jessica. He had spotted another cat named "Antony," an animal Peck was sure, once claimed, would scratch his eyes out. Peck bought hoops and tried to teach the cats to jump through them. He bought beachballs for the cats to push with their paws or sit on top of. But all they would do was puncture and pop the beach balls. He tried to teach them to chase coiled-up pipe cleaners. Or roll on their backs in crushed catnip. None of them would pedal the toy tricycle Peck bought at Woolworth's.

The next afternoon, Peck went where he had been hired. It was called the PussKat Lounge. He met the manager, who weighed four hundred pounds. "This is a promotional thing we're doing," said the manager whose name was Condon Jukes. "People think my name's Condom—but it's Condon," he said. Condon asked what kinds of cats performed in Peck's act. Ocelots? Jaguars? Peck said house cats. Condon looked skeptical. Well, whatever, he said, adding that he'd see Peck that evening about seven o'clock.

The motel and the strays made Peck feel lonely, probably because he called the cats by their names—Leslie, Russell, and Jessica—and missed the three people he'd felt close to. Jessica, of course, was the cat with the most confusing behavior. Still, she was the one Peck picked up repeatedly and held in his lap even though she repeatedly jumped off and dashed away.

The act was a success and a disaster. On the disaster side, the PussKat thrived primarily on rowdy drunks. It was where bosses took secretaries and secretaries picked up truckdrivers. Condon was frank: "We have an arrangement," he said, "with the motel next door." It was no place for a rookie with amateur cats. Leslie Fay, taken out of the carrier, stretched and purred.

50

She was happy to be stroked but had no ambitions beyond that. Russell walked on his hind legs while trying to bat a small tassel of yarn, but he did it when Peck was trying to get him to meow "Happy birthday to you." Jessica just bolted, shredding a man's polyester suit in the process and knocking over at least a dozen drinks. But the *magic* Peck performed between all the failed cat tricks stunned the room. He primed all the assembled and noisy drunks to expect to laugh at failure, then turned failure on its head with some effect that seemed, especially at so close a range, to be impossible. After the first night, Jessica fled altogether and the act became one of pretending to get either Leslie Fay or Russell to perform. The point, as Peck developed it, was to get the crowd laughing and booing and then to amaze them. In the third phase of his evolving routine, the gambit was to fail in some of the tricks himself, only to get one of the *cats* to perform it. Condon Jukes took Peck on for a second week, then a third, and his business doubled. He raised Peck's take to a hundred and thirty dollars a night. He offered to take Peck on full time, but Peck said no. He'd had enough. Even his hair was beginning to smell of cat urine. But in his three weeks at the PussKat, he began to formulate a theory. Peck began to think about the failure of expectations and whether one could build an act, perhaps even a lifetime, on such a principle.

And so he tried. His procedure in his post-college years, as he imagined them, living in New York, was what had landed him the cat job. He would hang out in the anterooms of fleabag talent agencies, and when he heard a call coming in, a talent hole that needed plugging, Peck would be there, saving some broken-down, chain-smoking, walking heart attack's life. He listened to wheezing voices through cracked doors say things like "Country & western singer? ... Country & western singer!

… What makes you think I'd have a country & western singer?" The phone would slam into its cradle and Peck's knuckles would be on the door, his head boyishly through the crack saying: "Excuse me, Mr. Fossbein … My name's Hank Peck. I'm a country & western singer … and I'm wondering …" Some blotched man with two days' stubble would say, "Don't move! Don't move!"

Peck bought and learned to play basic guitar in three days. He bought himself levis. He bought himself six bandannas, two pair of boots, and a jacket with fringe. He called his friend Russell, who was still at Bard trying to "see it out," as he said, and Russell came on down to the city and wrote eight songs in a key Peck could manage, satirical songs like "The Eighth Avenue Roundup" and "Who Will Buy My Squash Blossom." The songs were hits. Peck was a hit. He changed his costume to a three-piece suit with boots and a bolo. He made crust for the boots with papier-mâché to look like cowshit.

He used his guitar for magic, making flower bouquets and live birds appear out of the sound hole. He made cards disappear out of a patron's vest pocket to reappear lodged behind the strings. For a finale, Peck made the guitar itself disappear and sang his last song a capella to the final chorus when he'd reach his hands high into the air and—Presto!

Two years later, Peck's family finally tracked him down. Peck's new life had borne him somewhat like fast water, and it hadn't occurred to him that others might be wondering where he was or what he was doing, why he had never come home from Bard College after spring semester.

You can't just leave people. Who? *Someone* had said that.

The job Peck landed, where he had been for nearly four months at a steady two hundred dollars a night, was at a higher-class topless club. Peck decided to strip to the waist and show off two very large boobs painted on his chest. He strung his magic with a comedy routine about trying to make his boobs disappear, about how heavy they were. He incorporated large-chested and flat-chested women in the audience. He had about thirty running puns on themes like "keeping abreast" ("I kept a breast once..."). For his finale, Peck cued up a bump-and-grind record and salaciously *put on clothes* to the accompaniment—seven layers by the time the dance ended. He looked like one of New York's homeless.

One night in late October after Peck had recently turned twenty-one, he peered out through the milky haze of the bombarding theatrical lights to see his father. Dr. Peck came backstage after the show. His face wore both rage and dread.

"We meet again," his father said, his lip curled. Peck had never seen his father sneer. He looked like a caricature of himself, like someone else dressed as him on Halloween.

"I completely forgot," Peck said, as if he'd brought the family car home late from a date. "I completely forgot. I meant to call. I meant to write. I just got busy."

"Yes, indeed. *Busy! I can see!*" Dr. Peck said. He told Peck his brother, Nick, received a spinal injury in football his senior year at high school. His father didn't mince words. It was serious, he said, and there was doubt about whether Nick would walk.

Peck thought of his brother in the crook of his arm the last time he saw him, Nick upstairs with his nose against the window, and a slime of regret flushed from Peck's mind down into his throat.

"And I have to say," Dr. Peck added, his teeth clamped, "that Nicholas asked very specifically that you be informed, otherwise I wouldn't have even bothered looking for you."

Peck cleared his throat. He locked eye-to-eye with his father. "That's pretty harsh, isn't it—what you just said?"

"I feel harsh. I feel harshly—whatever," Dr. Peck said.

Peck sped to see his brother, who was remarkably upbeat despite the dire prognosis. Nick kept asking for Peck's news and saying how great it was he was doing so well. Peck said, "You'll get better." Nick said, "Probably not." Peck said, "Nicky, you're not listening. You'll get *better*. I'm telling you. That's a promise. I mean it."

Peck's and Nick's mother floated like an uncertain bird in the doorway to Nick's room, making soft liquid sounds. Peck said he wanted to move home, but Dr. Peck said he'd prefer that he not. In fact, Peck wasn't welcome, his father said. Peck said he'd take an apartment and work every day with his brother in physical therapy. Peck's father said, "What are you talking about? I'm the doctor. Why ...why? His injury has nothing to do with you."

"It has everything to do with me," Peck said.

Peck honored his promise. He got a room with kitchen privileges in Brookline, spent days with Nick. In the evenings, he performed free of charge at Mama G's in North Boston. Peck felt there was a connection. Every once in a while on a free morning or afternoon, he would walk into a classroom at Harvard and sit through a lecture on spectroanalysis or a discussion of Proust's verbs. Invariably the talk made no sense: twitching words dancing in the air, as Peck knew they would, like the mumbling of a shaman from a lost tribe. But Peck felt he should make the effort. He should try to sense whether he had walked away from something possibly valuable.

By January, Nick had his sensation back. By March, he

could raise and lower his legs slightly. By the following July, he took his first steps with the aid of a walker. On the anniversary of his injury, as a commuting student now to Harvard, Nick took his first rehabilitated steps—solo. *"Yes!"* Peck encouraged him. "Yes, Nicholas, yes! Fabulous! Do it! Go for it! I could whip your ass right now, one on one, but this is a good start!" Their mother cried. Dr. Peck attributed Nicholas's success to the *discipline* that had marked his progress. "He sets goals and he reaches them," he said. "Life has value for him."

Peck wished Nick well. He hugged his mother and was startled at how diminutive her frame felt, how frail this time, and husklike. He had traded his Subaru for a Land Rover. When he applied for plates, he requested six letters: REF NGE. No one else owned them. Dr. Peck handed him a book through the driver's window, *Don Quixote*, just before Peck pulled out. "Perhaps you'll find this instructive," he said. So Peck headed south again in his new *Refenge*mobile, twenty-two years old and in search of whether a lifetime might be built on the failure of expectations.

Five

hough Peck's funds were a bit depleted, he still had money in his bank account. He didn't have to find stray dogs, who could be relied on to shit on stage while he juggled tennis rackets, in order to buy his next meal or deposit two months' security on a new apartment, but he knew it was time to begin adding something back.

He canvassed Chelsea and Puerto Rican Harlem, where there were interesting studio flats, interesting neighborhoods. But in the end, he went back to Chinatown. Peck's explanation to himself was that he missed the clogging drift of black bean sauce and the glint of bad city light off the scales of carp. Again his room was above a restaurant, this time on Mott Street on the third floor. The restaurant was called simply Low's.

I'd call my agent now, Peck thought, *if I had one.* Instead, he drove up to Annandale to see Russell, who in his own helical way had been steadfast at Bard's and now was a senior. They had been writing. Peck had gotten the sense from the letters that Russell was depressed. Russell said he was gearing for the LSATs preliminary to all his applications to law schools. He also had the lead in Ionesco's *Rhinoceros,* in which he was so infused and transformed that he made Peck laugh and cry. "How can you be a lawyer?" Peck kept saying in Russell's dressing room while drinking Champagne afterwards. "How can you *do* that? It's a betrayal of your own talent!"

Russell made a vague gesture with his hand, knocking over the Champagne bottle, and fled out the door into a leafless Annandale night. Peck chased and found him. They walked, as they had two and a half years earlier, this time under a cold, naked sky. And they raged. They hugged one another. "I get scared," Russell confessed. "I get scared. I have thoughts." They found another student's guitar and sat together on the bank of the Hudson, singing in crude though not displeasing harmony the mock country & western songs Russell had written. "Damned law!" Russell said. "What am I doing?"

Peck heard an echo from the past, something from the inside of a car speeding away: *You can't just leave people.* He got Russell to pledge ongoing contact. "Don't get too low," Peck pleaded. "I'm not that far. I'm two hours away. Please."

Russell thanked him.

It seemed time for Peck to re-gather himself, to try to connect and knit up some loose threads of his past. Within forty-eight hours of his night with Russell, he boarded a plane to San Francisco, where he rented a Subaru for old time's sake and drove to Berkeley. At the undergraduate dean's office, he announced that he was Jessica Entemann's older brother and needed to find her. They scoured Jessica's records. Regarding a brother, they told Peck bluntly: "She doesn't have one."

"Look closer," Peck said.

"No brother," the administrator repeated.

"He's illegitimate," Peck said and left.

He tracked Jessica, from the public schedule listing, to an art history class. He walked in, the only light in the room spilling off a slide. It was of Picasso's harlequins, and it stopped Peck. He knew it. He'd seen prints. He'd seen it full-scale at the Metropolitan. A voice intoned about the picture's composition. The voice kept extolling Picasso's "theater of color and surface." *Theater of color and surface! Jesus, what a windbag!* The harlequin looked armed in the way only a performer can look armed and dangerous, Peck thought. He could steal your heart; he could steal his own; he could make both disappear.

Jessica was startled when Peck blocked her path out of the lecture hall. Her face turned red. She seemed confused and angry. She was with a young man who looked like he might be a mime, his skin was that ghostly. The young man's name was Terrence. He wore wire-rims and bound his hair in a pony tail. "I'm very busy," Jessica said. "This is a very busy time for me."

"All I'm asking is to take you out to dinner," Peck said.

"I have an hour exam and two term papers coming up," she said.

"I'll write them for you over dinner," he told her.

Terrence appeared the most uncomfortable of the three. Jessica finally agreed. She described where they should meet and at what time and then hurried away with Terrence.

"I named a *cat* after you!" Peck called to her retreating figure. She seemed not to hear.

When Jessica said she knew the perfect place to eat, Peck said he knew a better place and please get in the car. She did. "Where's this place?" Jessica said, the car rolling. "New York," Peck said, "Chinatown."

Jessica shrieked and threatened and swore for at least twenty minutes. She used words which Peck couldn't imagine coming out of her mouth. She scratched the right side of his face, drawing blood, and then apologized. She dabbed at the blood with a handkerchief. "Just tell me, just be honest," she said, "am I in danger?"

"What's your definition of danger?" Peck asked

He stopped in Reno for gas. After her swearing and fingernail attack, Jessica had gone on to tell him she had "heard all about him," what he'd done, what he'd done to his family, and what he'd done with his life. She recited a version which sounded like Peck's father's version, added to and embellished upon by the various authors of *Tales from the Crypt*. "I didn't know a person could be so cruel," Jessica said.

"Neither did I," Peck confessed.

She asked for his version of the story.

"Why?" Peck asked, then asked who Terrence was.

"A person who's very special," Jessica said.

"Why? Does he have a rare blood disease?" he probed.

In Reno, before he put her on a plane back to Berkeley, Peck bought Jessica dinner, a New York cut, at Harrah's. She said she didn't want a New York cut, then cried. And fumed. She told Peck he was not supposed to have appeared again in her life. Peck told her to never trust magicians. Before she vanished down a boarding ramp, she turned back and asked, "If I come to New York between semesters, can we talk?" Peck moved his jaw for the words, but he couldn't answer.

He found someone had slipped a message under his Chinatown apartment door to "Call Bard. Russell critical." It was hyperbole. When Russell got his LSAT scores back, and finding himself in the ninety-fifth percentile, his spirits had taken a plunge. He'd panicked and gotten drunk, tried calling his friend. Peck had not been in.

Russell found a pistol, stuck it in his mouth, and fired ...
except it was a starter's pistol. There were burns. There was
considerable pain. Russell said his mouth would always be a little larger. But he was fine. And when Peck finally made contact,
his friend seemed to have regrouped. "I figured it out," Russell
told Peck. "It's so easy. I figured it out! I'll be an entertainment
lawyer."

Jessica did not come to New York the following January.
Peck repeatedly called her at her Boston suburb home, but her
proper mother or dentist father would always ask, "May I say
who's calling?" and when Peck identified himself, as he did at
first, they would always say, "Jessica isn't here at the moment,
but if you would care to leave a number, ..."

The following August, Peck got an invitation to Jessica's
wedding ... to someone named Lewis Haseltine III. Peck kept
saying the name to himself, again and again, *Lewis Haseltine III
... Lewis Haseltine III!* He wanted to say to Jessica, "What's this,
did they try out two others before him?" Peck considered attending the wedding but rejected it. At least they hadn't asked
him to emcee. He thought about sending a gift, but then he
thought that if he sent a serious gift it would make Jessica mad.
If he sent a joke or something with a private message, she
wouldn't receive it. So, he pretended the invitation had gotten
lost in the mail.

Peck's own career moved like a tiny inchworm along an in-
cline which was only fractionally measurable. He got a regular
agent, Kelson Kopf, whose office was at the end of a dark corridor in a Russian neighborhood on Second Avenue on the lower
east side; Kelson Kopf, who when they met spotted Peck looking at him suspiciously and said, "I'm not a midget."

It was possible. It was possible the chair on which he sat was a child's chair. "I am not a midget," he repeated.

"It would be fine if you were," Peck said.

"What I am is your agent, if you'll let me be."

Peck felt relieved—or did he?

"What I'll be is your supporter, your fan, your advocate, your enthusiast."

Peck signed on.

And the Kelson Kopf Agency was not entirely a joke. Kelson managed Julio Ortega, who Peck had never seen live or even heard of but who about once a month in one capacity or another appeared on television, twice on the *Tonight* show. So, Kelson Kopf was real. He knew how to work the phones. And whoever they were, he had contacts.

Peck no longer had to do animal acts. He no longer had to work topless or stay in cheap motels in places like Hoboken. And he got paid. He was never entirely without money. He worked New York clubs, Philadelphia clubs, Atlantic City, Dallas, Reno. He worked on his theory of disappointed expectations, surprising audiences—pretending failure and then succeeding.

Failure, … abracadabra, … success! He moved the notion along for nearly five years, not exactly at breakneck speed, but it seemed a kind of template for his life. Almost always after a show, some bright person with a corkscrew brow, wearing a tweed jacket, would want to talk about what he had perceived to be his "performance concept." People would say he was very "individual" and had a "unique style"; they "hadn't ever seen anybody quite like him." So, with Kelson Kopf doing his scurrying in the background, Peck was always working. He rarely had an evening off. Still, activity and work notwithstanding, his future life and its *horizons,* given his pace and direction, opened its mouth across the Tappan Zee bridge, as it felt like most days, and yawned.

Meanwhile, Peck's brother, Nick, who had moved from being the invisible to being the visible son, built a new body through physical therapy and completed Harvard, only to go on to attack Harvard Medical School. There were days, if a person didn't know, that Nick was able to summon his legs to move him in such a way that no disability appeared. He felt hale. He felt frisky, and he felt loved. He was courting a consumer advocate named Lanie, and he told Peck it looked serious.

"How serious is *serious?*" Peck asked.

"When I think about her, I sweat," Nick said. "When she comes into the room, it's like fire floating on water."

Russell finished Columbia Law and took a job at—Peck could never get the name right, he always called it "Shalom and Yahweh"—a major Philadelphia law firm.

"How much entertainment law do they do?" Peck asked, "there in Independence Square?"

"You'd be surprised," Russell said. "There's a lot of good stuff happening in Philadelphia."

Peck's mother had a cataract operation. He flew to Boston and held her hand. His brother, Nicholas, introduced him to Lanie. She was bird-like, pale, insecure, but pretty, and Peck liked her. He could tell by the way Nick wrapped her in his long arm that things were indeed serious. Peck's father asked whether his son, the magician, had read *Don Quixote* yet.

There were, despite Kelson Kopf's dogged efforts and advocacy, some discouragements. One time at a reasonably respectable club in Brooklyn when Peck was producing pygmy owls, one after another from his fingertips, an inebriated patron scrambled onto the stage, unzipped his fly, and pissed on Peck's shin. Peck kicked him in the mouth and had to serve a five-day jail sentence.

While he was in jail, Peck met a mystic named Christo, who could slow his pulse to forty. Christo was into out-of-body however he could get it, even spending nights in large walk-in refrigerators to decrease his pulse and induce his spirit to wander. Peck found him intriguing. Everything he said seemed wrapped in one of the ice-blue, sealed-air blankets of packing boxes, and ultimately Christo himself seemed a kind of delusion. Peck wasn't sure, even sharing the same small cell, that he'd actually *met* him.

On the third night in jail, jackknifed into his cot, Peck dreamt that Antony Foley stood just beyond the hatched grate of the confining bars. Dangling keys and choked by hideous laughter, he'd become the new precinct sergeant. The dream seemed an opportunity, a challenge. Peck had been a worm once in Antony Foley's dreams; now Antony was a worm in his. The Antony worm seemed to be sneering and taunting: *Okay, smart guy; okay, big magician, show me your stuff!* Was Peck a man of magic or wasn't he? Was Peck an escape artist or not?

Peck wrenched himself from the dream and swung his naked feet, dropping them to the cement floor. He sat up. Christo was snoring. *Out-of-body, okay—out-of-body,* Peck started intoning to himself. He put his hands over his mouth, felt the least heat of his breath. He shut his eyes, imagined himself somewhere else ... *somewhere else ... somewhere else.* Where? He imagined Jessica, now Haseltine—was she *the third?*

He concentrated on slowing his breathing, dissolving it, until it was all but gone. He took his hands from his mouth. He stood. He could smell shag carpet and lavender soap and Tanqueray gin. He opened his eyes. ...

Perhaps he had never left his dream. Perhaps that was the explanation. Across the room, in whatever transport, dream, or legerdemain, two bodies slept on a vast bed. One had Jessica's unmistakable neck, undeniable shoulders. The other, with both arms wrapped around his pillow, was a stranger.

Peck closed his eyes again, slowed his breathing. He thought, *I need to be careful.* He sat. *I need to be very careful.* This time he mouthed the words, said them aloud so he might remember them. When he finally opened his eyes again for a third time, he was back in his cold, stone-smelling cell with the snoring Christo.

Two days later, in a different way, he was released. He was physically free.

Back in his apartment above Low's on Mott Street, three days after his release from the eighty-seventh precinct, a telegram arrived. "Dearest Peck—alert!" it said. It was signed Leslie Fay. But Peck had no more set the telegram down when his door imploded, kicked in, and two men in turtlenecks, carrying truncheons, entered and said, "This is from Mikey Fay."

"Show and tell!" one of them said as they descended on Peck.

When they left, Peck had two teeth hanging by threads. One eye wouldn't open. There were bones that needed to be set. The phone rang, and Peck, reeling, groped a hand toward it. It was Leslie in tears, apologizing. Her best friend, she said, Anita Gaye Fenniman, the sole confidante to hers and Peck's *reprieve,* had for whatever warped agenda *spilled the beans.* "I'm sorry," Leslie said. "Peck, I'm sorry. You were a kind of miracle, an innocent miracle, to me. *Say* something. I'm sorry."

It occurred to Peck that he might rethink his calling in life. There was something about magicians that compounded people's loathing. He felt the stickiness of his own blood, his clothes adhering to his skin like bad wallpaper. The paramedics, who finally came, kept intoning the word *phenomenal!* His father might have been right. Perhaps there were hidden clues (why hadn't he read the book yet?) in *Don Quixote.* Maybe he'd chosen his vocation prematurely, leapt toward what people call "the future" too recklessly. But what other possibilities were there that he hadn't already considered?

It took over a month before Peck tasted equilibrium, until his skin recovered from being the color of sheet metal and his eyes stopped looking like bloody yolks. His sense of balance struggled for a center. Every day, sometimes two or even three times a day, he called his brother, Nick, though without telling him what had happened.

"It's not that I mind," Nick said finally one day. "But this new thing—why are you calling me so much?"

"Hey, you're my brother, the doctor," was all Peck could think of to say.

"You could call your father, the doctor."

"Well, ..."

"And?—"

"And ... you're my brother. I don't know. You're my brother, that's all. The doctor. We talk and I feel better. Tell me you're not annoyed. Tell me life was easier for you when I left. Tell me to take two beautiful women and call you in the morning."

When Peck's equilibrium settled and his body mended, Kelson Kopf set him up for some television-series auditions.

"You look good as new!" he said. "Amazing! It's the shattering Peck trick. Now he's in pieces, now he's back together, brand new! You're the real Humpty Dumpty, my man."

Kelson Kopf had a strategy. Because Peck wasn't a kid any more, because he was twenty seven—*twenty-seven years old, boyo!*—Kelson believed the time had come to move past one-nighters and week-long engagements in city clubs and resort hotels. "Film and television! Film and television!" Kelson barked. His words rose somewhere between irritation and mantra. "You're going to audition and audition ... and then audition."

The auditions were, in fact, instructive. Some of the available parts even seemed remotely possible. Some seemed inspired. One director, seeing Peck twice for a possible series part, said in the spirit of professional advancement and support, "I don't know. You're somewhere between a star and an extra. I can't figure which."

Russell kept trying to set up meetings for Peck with film people, or more often friends of clients he was meeting through his law practice. "There's a new major film studio they're working on setting up in Toledo," Russell would say. "And this guy, who I'm going to arrange for you to have a drink with, is the brother of the guy who's the accountant. He says most of the money is practically in place."

And Peck would have the drink, or worse yet, buy the drinks for Russell's contacts between shows at some club where he was performing, and inevitably the person would turn out to be even more bizarre than his out-of-body cell mate, Christo.

There were women, too: new relationships, or near-relationships, more accurately, in what Peck considered to be his still youthful "discovery" years. Russell would fix him up with

Pennsylvania entertainers. Peck would call Jessica Haseltine III, now in West Hartford, to hear her voice and then hang up. It hurt him to think about Leslie Fay, that she'd spoken their secret and then seemed to seal herself off.

He tried girls for rent. He tried college students. He tried hopeful actresses, arrived out of high-school senior plays from Boise, Idaho, or Truces, New Mexico. It all seemed awful: dreadful, sick, opportunistic, calculating, and cruel. "Let me arrange a meeting with my agent, ..." he would say in a hideously glib voice that somehow, like a kestrel, came fluttering out of him. God! If Peck heard himself repeat that line once more, he would send *himself* to jail. He would put *himself* in some major hospital.

So, the confession had to be made that there were times, when hearing the dim reverb of his father's voice in some chamber of his brain (*riff-raff!*), Peck would wonder if he had in fact missed a turn; had he simply never seen it? He went back to Boston for the holidays and tried to be polite to the gathered friends of the family, doctors and their wives, who over "wassail" interrogated him as to how he was doing. He would try, always, to present himself as assured and undefended until his father would step forward to torpedo the flimsy balsa boat of Peck's buoyancy.

"My son says he's in the arts, but that's stretching it."

Peck, in return, would add, "Dad says they've asked him to be Chief of Staff. I think he'd be great."

Perhaps it was at those times, mostly, when Peck began to reflect and wonder about marriage. He looked at his family and saw no visible seams in his parents' marriage. It seemed unmarked by division. And yet, ... and why did he keep wanting to say *and yet*? Probably because under a microscope, Peck's parents seemed to be citizens of separate countries. In his father's country, people were precisely carved out of marble. In his mother's country, people were made of reflected light. In his father's country, you knew who you were. In his mother's country, you wanted to hold the elusive light in your hand because it all seemed so warm and magical, and yet ...

Was his parents' marriage the ideal of what "life together" was supposed to be? Was it intended to be stone and tremulous light? His parents were model parents, he'd been told, his family a model family. Nick had announced his own marriage. "Guess what? Lanie and I are going to tie the knot in April, and we want you to be the best man." So, Peck raised the question with Nick. "Is there something I'm not getting here?" he asked, "about the folks? About what their ..." (the word he kept hearing people use was *dynamic*) "dynamic is?"

Nick laughed. "No, c'mon. You need to lighten up." He said Peck thought too much, that it was just their parents' generation; that was the way they all were. Look at the other doctors and their families.

So, Peck looked. Then he stopped looking. Or at least, he shifted his gaze to Nick. He was proud of what he saw. Nick seemed to have left little-brotherhood behind. He seemed astute. His brother was going to join the ranks—take the plunge. Probably there was such a thing as a good marriage. Probably there was love.

Peck himself had felt a serious caring for two women in his life, hadn't he? There was the one he'd held close on the dance floor and one he'd shared a bathtub with. Hadn't he known a kind of affection and caring, of touch?

It seemed so long ago that Peck had been an eleven-year-old, for whom all futures seemed possible. Now he was a twenty-seven-year-old, for whom any kind of tomorrow seemed indeterminate. How, exactly, had that happened? How did one even temporarily misplace the notion that all a person needed to do was dare to perform a trick? Until he was seventeen, or even eighteen, it seemed all that was necessary was to dare to imagine. If he could imagine it, then whatever—money, flowers, love from a woman—*presto!*—it appeared or disappeared, didn't it? If he just performed the trick.

But since then, ... now ... had he grown careless or something? Had he been jinxed? Had he, some drunken, reckless night, spilled the beans? *A magician never tells.* ... Had he broken a trust? Told a trick?

Apparently not. Happily within a week, two events returned Peck to the path of his earlier arrogance and the delicious rewards of what Dr. Peck often called his son's defiance. His career catapulted, and he fell in love.

The career vault had the feel of fire again—*flash paper* at Peck's fingertips. His blood eddied and crashed. Back again into his realm of influence rushed an empowering limitlessness which, in the ninth grade, he'd felt when he had mesmerized young Conley Pfeiffer into his plate of creamed chicken, when the school's administration begged him to wake his classmate up and bring him out. The love, on the other hand, almost escaped him, it was so unadorned and quiet.

Six

W hat happened with Peck's career was a half-hour comedy series called *Making Due,* which dealt with a group of young people working in a collection agency. Kelson Kopf, sending him into the first audition, had called it a long shot. He said such series usually knew who they wanted before they cast. Still, "Look, it's America!" and if Peck had "the balls he was born with" and went the next day to the thirteenth floor ("Don't be superstitious!") of a building on West 57th Street between Broadway and Eighth Avenue, someone in an office there named ("Just a minute, I wrote this down") *Lisa Cantrell* would have *sides* for him, scene pages. He should take the sides, take them home; he should look them over that night. The following day, he'd have a twenty-minute slot to make his case on the twenty-sixth floor of a building on Fifth Avenue on the corner of 49th Street. "I essentially had to sell *my dick* to get you this audition," Kelson said, "but the way things have been going in my life, it's an unnecessary appendage. So, enjoy ..."

Peck took a breath and thanked his agent.

He'd run similar obstacle courses previously. It was practically rote. He caught a cab at the corner of Mott and Canal and taxied to the appointed Westside building, where he "charmed" Kelson's Lisa Cantrell, when she gave him his pages, by producing a 42-D brassiere out of her blouse. It was, Peck understood, a risk—a kind of throwback to his topless days. Still, magic was magic; it had brought him to life. Peck trusted it. There was such a thing as the *wrong trick*. Peck, who had just said *Voila!* stood with the bra in one hand, the audition pages in the other. Lisa Cantrell, like a stoplight, turned orange, red. She made theatrical sounds of humiliation and kept moving her tongue against her upper lip to check its placement. Finally, though, she smiled, her teeth white and flat and reflective enough to be a mirror. "Good luck!" she said to Peck. And she repeated it. "Good luck."

Peck read the sides. The dialogue made his brain bend. Who wrote for television, anyway? Who *were* these people and what kind of training did they have, doing stock inventories for department stores? These particular sides, though particularly terrible in certain stretches, were not as bad as some he had seen. They were punctuated correctly, which counted for something. And there was a line which Peck quite liked. In response to a co-worker's, "Did you have a date last night?" Peck's character replied, "They hadn't dried yet."

This character he would be auditioning to play was basically a repo man, someone who had grown up blue-collar, his father a plumber, and arrived in the suburbs deputized to take back appliances such as garbage disposals, dishwashers, and soft water conditioners when the payments had gone too far into arrears. Water seemed to be the common denominator in all of the character's retrievals. If it wasn't plumbing, it was a waterbed. The character was also a compulsive letch, trying to strike endless suggestive deals with the women from whom he was retrieving appliances. In one of the scenes, the character, once inside the door, came on tactlessly, to which the behind-in-payments housewife—sounding not unlike Jessica Entemann—pleaded, "Take your hand off my shoulder. Go away. Take the disposal!"

Peck memorized his scenes. The next day he went to the twenty-seventh floor. A receptionist who looked like Lisa Cantrell's older sister but wore better clothes said things were backed up and would he wait? Given the running gags on water, Peck considered making a plumbing joke about being backed up, but then thought better of it.

Finally the call came to read. "Mr. Peck?" A blue door led him into a small office. Three men and a woman sat on chairs of oiled wood and gray tweed fabric. One man was the series director, a Jack Gilson. The others had industry titles. They introduced themselves as the producers, associate directors, sponsors. The word *network* was repeated.

A man and a woman, both looking very familiar, were called in from yet another anteroom. Introductions were made, and Peck read with them. Afterward, one of the producers began to thank him, when the director, Jack Gilson, asked, "Could we hear him read again?"

Peck did so. Again he got thanked. The next day, Kelson Kopf called. "They want you to read for another of the characters," he said. "This is favorable."

Peck greeted Lisa Cantrell, who delivered new sides.
"No bra this time?" she asked, white teeth flashing.
"I'm trying to be mature," Peck said.
Lisa looked disappointed.

"I've been told I should grow out of my lingerie phase," Peck tried.

"Not forever, I hope," Lisa said.

They parted.

Peck read over and prepared his new material. This time his character was a Harvard Business School graduate "slumming" it in order to gather material for a book called *Credit & Consequence.* The character's name was Ethan Frost. His character bit was that he was smart, (surprise!) he was stupid. *Ha-ha.*

Peck read for Ethan. Again, Jack Gilson asked him to re-read. And again the next day, Kelson Kopf called Peck, saying the series wanted him to return for yet a third character. "I don't want to get your hopes up," Kelson said, "but this has never happened where a client didn't get an ongoing guest role, at least."

This time the character was a blond California surfer. It was a stretch to imagine how a surfer guy had taken a job as a New Jersey loan-collection officer, but the "read" on him was he was the one they sent out of state to try to make the more difficult and far-flung delinquencies right. Given his passion for Malibu, he was always trying to get to California. Of course, he always ended up going to places like Bismark, North Dakota.

This time, when she flashed her teeth, Peck asked Lisa Cantrell out. "Tonight?" she said. "I'd love to!" And so they did, and Peck ended up sleeping with her. Well, not exactly sleeping. Lisa got drunk, and he took her home and put her to bed. He sat up in a chair memorizing lines because for some reason there was broken glass on the floor and Peck was worried Lisa would stagger up for a trip to the bathroom and slice open her foot. When she did wake, she smiled dreamily at Peck, who had cleaned the glass up and was making coffee. Her voice was husky, but she purred, "It was a wonderful date, incredible for me." Peck left and bleached his hair, and that afternoon he did his third audition. He felt appropriately at sea. On his way out, he heard a producer stage-whisper to another, "Listen to him. He's the guy!"

Then Jack Gilson stopped him. "Word is you do tricks!"

Tricks—whoops! Had Lisa Cantrell called? She had, but only to express delight about Peck's magic. Peck talked briefly about his background. He briefly outlined his personal theory of life from failed expectations.

Interesting.

Yes, interesting.

He left them nodding their heads.

The committee of producers and directors tried him for the three remaining principal characters. One was black and two were women. In each case, still, there was the murmured, *Jesus, he is this … person.* With the women's parts, he stayed on while the group debated transvestites, whether they were funny or not. A sponsor questioned the idea (he called it a *concept*) that no one had ever done a series with drag. Another producer pronounced her own considered opinion that cross-dressing was inherently funny: "Use a cross-dresser in a series and you have a hit." Peck was not exactly feeling buoyed about his life by their considerations.

But then came the final callback with no sides at all. *A mute!* Peck speculated about what this could mean. "Listen to this!" he was instructed. Jack Gilson had come up with what they thought was an absolutely amazing concept for Peck's character. Jack's concept was that there should be a new character with the following background. "Listen carefully," Peck was told. The new character would come from Boston and be the son of a doctor, someone with a disabled brother, Gilson said. "He does magic. He does comedy. He's been a kind of *wunderkind* ... a bit with women, a bit with life in general. On the one hand, he's an innocent; on the other, he's got nerve ... but he's in a kind of trough now, a low, a depression. He's struggling to pick *the magic* up all around, and his temporary solution is his work in this office."

Peck nodded.

"Man alive!" The five other faces in the room cocked forward and shone like brass. "Tell us what you think!"

"Tell us what you think!" two others shouted, obviously juiced with enthusiasm.

Peck tightened his teeth. His jaw muscles leapt in a kind of rhythm as he nodded. Finally, he pronounced the new character concept workable. He could relate, go along with nearly everything but the disabled brother. Peck asked Jack where the specific notion had been born.

"It just came to me," Jack Gilson said. "It was just one of those things ... just sort of *flew in,* I don't know, from different pieces."

"So then, like to an air traffic controller," Peck said.

"Sometimes you just get lucky," Jack said. "Sometimes you're creative."

"What's the character's name?" Peck asked.

"*Name.* Absolutely right. *A name.* Did we come up with a name?" Jack Gilson, one by one, polled the others.

They hadn't.

"Wait a minute! Wait a *minute!*" Jack Gilson's face shone like a 120-watt bulb. "This is brilliant!" he said.

"Include me in. I can keep a secret," Peck said.

"What if we use *your* name?" Jack Gilson said.

"My name?"

"Perfect!" one of the show's producers said. "*Perfecto!*" he added for emphasis. "We'll call the character Peck."

Peck was offered the job. It wasn't unexpected. Jack Gilson seemed to have a special appreciation when Peck accepted. Kelson Kopf was ecstatic. He had never had a client, he said, who had actually climbed the ladder to a television series and "stardom." The pay was substantial. Peck was immediately put on contract, then given two weeks off before start-up rehearsal time.

He thought of calling his parents, sharing his news, but resisted. His mother, he felt, would be reflexively happy, his father reflexively glum, saying something like, "So, now what? You're a celebrity?" Neither of them would understand.

It was hard. Peck wanted to feel some larger world embracing his good fortune. He was twenty-eight now—twenty-eight years old! There should be calls to make, people to gather for dinner. He called Russell in Bucks County.

"Fabulous!" Russell said. "Fabulous!" He was drunk.

Peck asked why he'd been drinking. Had he dined with clients, had he been at a party?

"I don't know," Russell said. "A person opens a bottle of Chivas and pours it over ice and it's a mystery, it's profound. I don't know, no reason."

Peck asked how Russell's job was going.

Russell said, "Shitty," and then added, "Hey, I'm kidding."

Peck outlined the character he was to portray, and he and Russell laughed, point by point. They giggled. "Gosh, they nailed you," Russell said. "They *nailed* you, every nose hair. Peck plays Peck. Great!"

Russell wanted to get into his Spider, drive to New York, and buy Peck a drink. Peck discouraged him. "I could've been a star!" Russell said. "This guy, me. I could've been a contender."

"Hey, you are," Peck kept saying. "Hey, buddy, you are! You're a contender. Don't undersell yourself. You're a contender all the way."

Russell asked Peck to listen to three new songs he'd written, and sang them over the phone between hits on his scotch.

Peck cringed at the gaps for scotch but otherwise beamed. The songs were good, and he said so. Someday, Peck said, a lot of people will be singing Russell's songs.

"So, why did I do this?" Russell asked, far more drunk than when they'd begun. "Why did I go to where I am, this place … where is it anyway? What's it called? Oh yeah, *law. Hey, I'm just kidding!*"

Peck hung up and felt bad. He called Leslie Fay at her home, but when she lifted the phone he couldn't speak with her. He called Jessica in West Hartford and barely let the phone ring. Peck wondered how many times do people *do* that: call people they care about but break the connection before caring becomes possible?

He called his brother's beeper at the Peter Bent Brigham Hospital in Boston where he was doing a radiological residency. "Nick, guess what?" Peck began, and then told his story. Nick kept saying, "Alright! Alright!" The two laughed. They invented spins on their parents' possible reactions. Nick, married now eight months, told Peck Lanie was pregnant. "We're *on the moon*," he said, his voice aquaver he was so happy. "We just can't bloody believe it. Peck, it's incredible! We're *on the moon* with this!" When they closed their call, Peck was filled with a kind of gratitude for his brother and what they shared. But he was filled with a terrible loneliness as well.

So, instead of gathering friends, rather than being touched

by the pride of parents, Peck's rather muted job celebration involved descending his apartment stairs and taking dinner alone at Low's, the noodle house and restaurant occupying the first floor. At his corner table, he felt sadly small. He was a curious phantom haunting the edges of the restaurant. At twenty-eight, on the day of his breakthrough, he was his own ghost—pale and insubstantial.

It was okay, he guessed. Twenty-eight wasn't old by any stretch. There was time. Life was nothing if not possibilities. Low's shiny menu stood before him. He decided to go for broke and order the Hunan lobster, duck noodles, and start off with some sizzling rice soup.

Low's was always busy. The Gow family, who owned and ran it, were remarkable, exquisite cooks. There was almost always a ready crowd, a dozen or more student- and graduate-student types milling around the coatrack at the front. In warm weather on weekends, the hopefuls spilled out onto Mott Street. The Gows knew Peck. He was already a celebrity of sorts to them because he'd performed there a few nights, free of charge. Mrs. Gow would sometimes call him back into the kitchen to taste a special dish.

The Gows' daughter, Victoria, waited tables, and she soon became the second of Peck's two turnaround events—falling in love. She had a hushed and quietly beautiful way about her. She was perhaps twenty-four and always dressed in a modest sweater and black skirt, with little makeup. Her neck was long, her eyes enormous and reserved. Intelligence spanned her brow. There was a kind of heat in her lips. Peck knew her to the degree that they had spoken. He had teased. She had responded, always shyly, taking his order, bringing his food, filling his water glass and tea, bringing his check. He would always tip. It had been ceremonious and casual.

Tonight, though, Peck watched her differently as she left his table, and wondered where the difference lay. Was it in her moving away ... or in his watching? When she brought the sizzling rice, he asked if she had always worked for her parents.

"No," she said.

Peck remembered that she had not been there when he first moved in above them. Had she always lived in New York?

"I lived in Cambridge, Massachusetts, briefly," Victoria said.

Peck confessed Cambridge to be his home—or home ground—near it, anyway.

When she brought the duck noodles, Peck asked what she had been doing in Cambridge. Had she been going to school? Victoria said yes, she had been at Radcliffe. Peck re-evaluated. Certain of her mystery came together, added up, made its sense. Had she graduated, Peck asked. Victoria said she had attended three semesters. "My family needed me to work here," she said, "so I came back." Peck asked what she'd been studying, primarily. "Organic chemistry and philosophy," she said. She liked to read and still "read a great deal."

It made Peck think, made him re-evaluate. He felt an unstable stirring in himself and was unsure what it meant. When Victoria brought his Hunan lobster, he asked whether she would consent to go for a walk after Low's closed that evening. She said, "Thank you, that would be nice," and reset a finished table.

In his room, waiting for the restaurant to close at eleven, Peck kept having the taste of almond on the roof of his mouth and sensing Victoria. On a yellow pad, he tried to write the formula for his life to that date, that which had brought him the deepest heat of mystery and what seemed to hold that heat at bay. At the top of the sheet, he wrote "Making failed expectations pay." Under that, he wrote Roman numeral I and headed it "Three Secrets of Magic." Under A, B, and C, he listed:

A. Into the void
B. Out of the void
C. The divination of secrets.

Something, Peck felt, was at last making a kind of sense. Roman numeral II was headed "My Life So Far," under which came:

A. What's supposed to happen doesn't.
B. What's not supposed to happen does.
C. When the trick seems to have failed, and it's over, suddenly, without words or warning, it works.

Peck memorized his yellow sheet and recited it again and again. He mumbled the phrases. *What's supposed to happen doesn't. What's not supposed to happen does.* Something was alive in the notations. Something was imbedded, hidden. It was a kind of riddle.

At eleven, he descended to Low's and found Victoria. He detected subtle eye shadow and lip gloss. Her family, she said, would be finishing the closing.

In the New York dark, the two walked across Canal and up Green Street. Peck asked a hundred questions, and Victoria's answers, each time, figured richer and more complex patterns in a kind of deepening crystallography of conversation. Peck felt amazed. How had the evening not happened earlier? There was a kind of trembling in him about it all; their arms would brush in the walking and he would feel it at the base of his skull.

Before they stopped for a drink, Peck was in love. After their first Chenin Blanc, Peck felt lost and giddy. Victoria opened. She laughed, although it was unlike any laugh Peck had ever known. It made no sound. Her lips would press and seem, in doing so, to move some emotion out from dead center. Her eyes would do something that reminded him of blossoms opening. There would be a flaring of her nostrils, a lift of her neck. It seemed boisterous and pure grace, both at once. Peck was enraptured and reordered wine to keep asking endless questions. Whatever he asked, she answered in the most exquisite and endearing way. He discovered, for instance, that each semester Victoria took a course in the city at Columbia. That way, by the time she was thirty, she would have her degree. At her door, on returning, Peck asked, "May I ... put my arms around you?" Her raised lips seemed to reach up and take his in. Climbing his stairs, Peck found he was shaking.

They began dating as though it had been going on for years. Peck called Russell at lunch hour so as to not catch him drunk. He confessed, "I'm in delirium." "My friend, my friend!" Russell said and began to cry. That night, Peck's phone rang. There was a piano introduction and a love song, "Only for You," which had been written, Russel said, for his friend. Peck went to the Gows. "Teach me how to chop bok choy," he said.

So, Peck began his new series and spent his free time with Victoria, somehow falling *into the void, out of the void,* and discovering *the divination of secrets.* The series bloomed. It was a success—the network's number one Thursday-night program. Peck's picture began appearing in the television digests and commentaries. Some credited Peck's particular kind of zaniness with being the heart and the pleasure of *Making Due.* One reviewer wrote: "When you most expect him to appear in a scene, he doesn't. When he's least expected, *Voila!* Often he botches a problem impossibly, but then *Presto!* The impossible happens—and of course in his own quirky way, which all makes sense."

Peck, in fact, scripted some of the moments the reviewer cited. Peck had middle-of-the-night and out-of-the-blue inspirations, which he converted into turns and spins on scripts. He became a master of the spur-of-the-moment, inventing on set and keeping the cast lively. He used Russell's songs on the show and got Russell paid for them. One day, feeling particularly frisky and within a rush, he called his father's Boston office. "Please, it's critical," he told his father's secretary. "Mrs. Breed, it's critical. Interrupt him." When his father took the phone, he said in a clearly breathless voice, "Now you can start using the word!"

"Who—" Peck could sense a faltering in his father's voice. "Who is this? Is this you, Peck? Use the word? What do you mean! What word?"

Something cautioned Peck: *Don't be haughty. Don't be arrogant.* But he couldn't help it. "Celebrity," he said. "You can use the word *celebrity.*"

Dr. Peck vanished into a silence.

"Pop?" Peck questioned.

"Has Nicholas? ... Has Nicholas called you?" Dr. Peck asked.

Peck said no, what? ... Why? Had Lanie delivered?

"Early this morning," Dr. Peck said.

"And?"

"A boy. Eight and a half pounds. 'Willie.'"

"And it all went well? ... *Tell* me, okay? Lanie's alright? The baby's okay? ... 'Willie' ... No complications?"

"He's short a finger on each hand," Dr. Peck said.

What was his point? Peck wondered. What was the response to the news his father thought Peck should have? "So, what?" Peck said. "Should I buy him a catcher's mitt?" *Bad response. Tacky impulse.* He hated himself for that.

In celebration, Peck called Lanie's room at the hospital and found Nick was there. Nick held the phone out for Peck to listen to the background sound of "nursing," or "live nursing," as Nick said. He spoke of Willie's hands. They were more beautiful than five-digit hands, he said. But Peck began to cry. He heard Nicholas announce to Lanie, "He's crying!" She laughed, then started to cry herself. Nick cried. "The baby's the only one not crying," Nick said. The two brothers said they loved each other and hung up.

Peck wanted to send Lanie a gift for making his brother so happy, for delivering life, for enabling Peck himself to envision design. He called her room back, asked Nick to put her on the phone.

"She's a little woozy," Nick said.

"I like woozy," Peck returned.

"Hey," Lanie's voice said—sounding a bit like Styrofoam mid-ocean.

"Tell me something you need," Peck requested.

Lanie giggled.

"No, really, something you need. Something you never thought you'd have but you've dreamed of. Name it."

That night Peck called his father at home and apologized for his flippancy. His father seemed at a loss. It seemed there was something his father wanted to speak to Peck about but didn't have the words for.

"We *say* things," his father said.

"And *do* things," Peck confessed.

"Say hello to your mother," his father urged.

Peck's mother's voice came on the phone. "Peck?" it said. It was a voice like the most fragile glass, like the softest feathers, like light.

"How're you doing?" Peck said.

Like a broken field runner, Peck's luck charged forward. All around him was daylight. His luck galloped. Another avenue opened. A new adventure! A syndicated radio program, which was a comedy and variety show, in essence the current decade's version of burlesque and vaudeville, asked him to be a weekly regular. His bit was to do magic tricks on radio.

His line on the radio became, "Now, watch my hands!" One week he emptied Lake Mead: "Now, I'm just going to put this handkerchief over Lake Mead ..." The next week, using existing tapes, he changed the incumbent president into Teddy Roosevelt and then back into Jimmy Stewart. "Whoops!"

Of course, outside the extended hours of his career, it was Victoria and Peck, Peck and Victoria. He studied her language. One week he gave all his lines on *Making Due* in Chinese. It was a sensation. He learned to cook. He learned Tai Chi. He studied geography and the era of Chinese communism. He began to peruse books on organic chemistry, even tried reading Schopenhauer. He loved the Gows, and they seemed fond of him, except that Mr. Gow would sometimes wonder aloud, "I don't know ... be good thing ... for Victoria marry a ... Peck."

Lord, Lord, Lord—he loved Victoria! He loved that people paid him to be delirious! He loved it that, even though it was radio, he could make whole land masses appear and disappear.

So, even though he was moving up on thirty, it seemed to Peck that he was eleven again.

Seven

eck brought Victoria home.

He had rambled, long distance, to both his parents and, of course, to Nicholas: *Victoria ... Victoria ...* His father, on hearing of her, had seemed removed, as though his mind were on some patient's history or lab tests. His mother had seemed either too enthused or too adrift and manufacturing of cheer. If Peck's two parents were shores, then something seemed irregular on the bridge. The river was aflood. *Something.* Peck knew his parents, and such as it was, their rhythm seemed off. There appeared no spark in all the coding that was familiar.

They flew to Boston. Peck drove a Mercedes now, but flying seemed easier. Nick met them. He'd put on weight. He wore a wrinkled wool suit and bore his two-year-old, eight-fingered Willie on his shoulders. "This is so fantastic!" he said. "This is so unbelievable!" And then Nick held Victoria at arm's length, one arm on each of her shoulders, and said: "Hey ... you seem ... *nice,*" and "this is *good.* This is so unbelievable!"

"Nicholas! Jesus, what did you expect?" Peck said.

Nick picked up Lanie in Lexington and the five drove to the

family house. Peck had spelled Victoria's name: G ... o ... w, though never thought it necessary to spell out the issue of race. Nick, certainly, had not seemed surprised, nor had Lanie. Willie played—his four-fingered hands like little birds—nonstop with Victoria's hair. The two couples laughed and rambled as though they had spent half a lifetime together. Their parents met them at the front door and wore smiles, but some chemical had been left out of the developer. Their images appeared washed and queerly frozen.

"Greetings," Peck's mother said. "Welcome." Her usual warmth seemed distracted, askew. Dr. Peck shook Peck's hand and took Victoria's coat, but he couldn't find a sequence of words.

They sat in front of the fire and had Dubonet with chilled shrimp and cocktail sauce. Chopin etudes romped in crisp fidelity in the background. The talk was of recent troubles at the Fine Arts Museum and of how Joyce Chen's had gone down hill as a restaurant. It all seemed curiously oblique, close to surreal, to Peck. They ate their dinner of lobsters and steamers. Nick tied everybody's bib. Willie threw red cartilaginous shells against the Audubon wallpaper. Peck's mother seemed either too delighted or too sad.

That night, after all the others had gone to bed, only Peck and Dr. Peck stayed in the study watching late-night television.

"Do you ever watch yourself?" Peck's father asked. The inquiry, Peck saw, had something to do with performing through the medium of television.

"I'm sorry; what's the question?" Peck said.

"You didn't tell us," his father leveled.

Peck ran with the bait. "I didn't tell you ... I'm sorry, what?" he said.

"That, uh ..." Peck's father couldn't finish his sentence.

"Yes?" Peck said.

"Don't be coy," Peck's father cautioned.

Peck smiled. He roiled. He felt angry. He was not his father's child anymore, but they'd done that, they'd re-negotiated those issues. "Do you want me to punch you in the mouth?" Peck tried.

"Some of our best anesthesiologists are oriental," Dr. Peck offered.

"Some of our funniest entertainers," Peck said, "are doctors."

"I don't mean to be intolerant," Peck's father said.

"Well, we succeed sometimes when we feel least ordained," Peck managed.

"So, are you sleeping with her?"

"How about you and mother? Are you making it once a week or so?"

Dr. Peck left the room.

Peck felt bad. Anger was never an answer.

The next morning at breakfast, Peck's mother asked Victoria if she were French. Victoria said yes. Peck later, privately, asked: "What was *that*?" Victoria said, "I just wanted your mother to feel comfortable."

Peck felt he'd stumbled into a different house. Certain fundamentals had been misplaced. *Successful son brings chosen girl home to meet parents.* Wouldn't that be the headline? Wasn't the scenario supposed to be one of joy and indulgence? "It's all right," Victoria said. "I understand closed groups." They flew back to La Guardia the third day, and Peck wondered, if they caught a return shuttle and tried again, if this time the pieces wouldn't fall into their proper places.

Peck and Victoria, truth given its moment, weren't in fact sleeping together. Had Peck answered his father, he would have had to admit this. It was different for Victoria. Something seemed forestalled. If *forestalled* wasn't the right word, Peck thought, *pending* would touch a certain truth. They lay together, outstretched on Peck's bed in scant clothes, sometimes undergarments. Peck could feel his slightest bodyhair strike Victoria's, and hers his. They would kiss one another's lips, one another's shoulders and eyes. Union seemed always possible, never disallowed, sometimes imminent. It just seemed to hold its breath, so to speak.

Are you sleeping together?

No, so to speak. Back in New York, Peck thought he might have made that answer. *No, we lie awake, so to speak.*

In fact, they had talked about it. "Is this strange," he would say, "what we do ... don't do with each other? That we're this intimate but aren't? That we've never ... Help me. I'm running out of ways to ask this question."

"I don't think it's strange," Victoria said. "It's never seemed strange to me."

"Okay," Peck said. "I just thought it would be ... you know, good to ask the question."

Victoria made a crescent with the tip of her tongue under one of Peck's eyes.

One of the more wonderful levels of craziness in Peck's work on *Making Due* was another cast member, J.T. Dennis. J.T. was a storm cloud. An Irishman like Peck, he was black and brooding, having landed in the world loosely called "entertainment" by a kind of default. He looked like a bitter Golden Gloves contender with a pommeled nose and an uneven face, hair that appeared sewn on when he wasn't attentive to it. His face looked chafed. His father was a high-ranking officer in the air force, so J.T. had shuttled around Europe and Asia the way other kids wander around an amusement park. He'd gone to American schools, an American college in Bern, and thought at first he'd be a translator and code breaker. But he deciphered one message that so infuriated him, he wouldn't reveal its contents and quit.

He then returned to the U.S. and had gone to the University of Maryland, where he'd gotten a degree in genetics. "I thought I'd splice genes," he told Peck. "I'd spliced words and wires—hell, why not?" When he saw the people "at the cutting edge" were "like kids playing with Lego, ... I was out of there." He'd driven a cab. He'd been a programmer. He'd played semi-pro hockey for a year. He'd tamed animals, done makeup and special effects; he'd sung backup on an Art Garfunkel album.

"Then I had a friend who was an actor at Yale or Juilliard or somewhere, all that shit. He was going up for an audition. He was basically a dickhead, I thought—about as emotional as a duck. So I went to the audition, too. I said I'd been acting for ten years in regional theaters. Obviously, I mean, here I am. It's history."

Peck adored J.T. "Let's face it," J.T. said, "we're the proton and electron nucleus of this operation."

J.T. stirred things up. He didn't exactly cotton to the director, Jack Gilson, whom he called "Peck's patron." He liked to loose live animals in the studio. There'd be a mandrill monkey tipping over equipment or a terrified kudu, its feet constantly going out from under it on the waxed tiled floors. One day when Jack arrived to set up the show, there was a full-sized live tuna flopping on the studio floor and sucking for air. J.T. apparently knew a zoo exchange and outlet nearby in New Jersey. Only Peck had been let in on this particular secret terrorism. "It reminds me of when I first broke into the business," Peck confided, and he thought of his cats.

Always, though, J.T. was a man of passion and fury. When he fell in love, it was thermonuclear. He'd be depressed, he'd be jealous and anxious and even vengeful. Unless the woman were within sight, he would be sure she had flown away, never to return. He imagined rivals, dismantling J.T. in the process, his stability and talent. When someone J.T. was seeing wouldn't answer his phone call, he'd invariably rip a phone box off the wall or a phone out of its base.

Being successful only made things worse. Invariably an envelope of bills arrived at the producer's desk with a typed note, "For the baby water buffalo damage." Once Peck accompanied J.T. to the apartment of a girl who had broken off their relationship. "I need you to protect me from myself," J.T. said. When the girl refused to listen to him, J.T. put both fists through the plaster on either side of her head. When Peck chastised him in the elevator, J.T. said, "Don't worry. I could never hurt a woman."

Peck's friend was also a money machine. *Making Due* only gave him more capital to work with. On the side, he bought run-down cooperatives to restore. If a wall needed to come down, he would personally take a sledge-hammer to it and bring it down in minutes. "Union goons!" he'd say. "Who needs them?" He ripped plumbing and wiring out bare-handed. He would film all day, then sheet-rock and paint and tile and wire most of the night.

He bought a trashed top floor on Columbus Avenue for $120,000 and sold it five weeks later, with a skylight, for $200,000. One February he bought two cooperatives, side by side, in a building just off Gramercy Park for a combined price of $420,000. He took out the pain of yet another failed relationship on the project and was a rebuilding madman for seven weeks. Then in mid-April he sold it as a lavish and spacious single dwelling for just under a million. "This fucking money is so easy to make, it's silly," J.T. said.

Making Due lasted five years. Peck and Victoria got married in a Buddhist temple at the beginning of the third year, with their reception, of course, hosted by The Gows at Low's. Peck performed at his own reception, utilizing food objects. He strolled the tables, reaching suddenly into the blue-white light to find dim sum, holding them like billiard balls between all his fingers. He swirled a red table cloth like raw pizza crust over an empty serving cart and then *out of the void,* Peking Duck! Russell and J.T. and Peck sang Beach Boys and Everly Brothers songs, as well as Russell's compositions. They did hilarious impressions in singer combinations: Dean Martin, Frank Sinatra, and Sammy Davis Junior; George Burns and John Denver; Willie Nelson, Dolly Parton, and Pavarotti. People sang in Yiddish. People sang in Chinese. Peck may have made his parents uncomfortable when he led the entire party in an old Congregationalist hymn, "A Mighty Fortress," but it seemed right for the occasion.

Peck may have made his parents generally uncomfortable, but they arrived uncomfortable. There was that same strange patina of graciousness, an almost ethereal formality, until Peck could see his mother was drunk. She was *very* drunk. His father was trying to mask it by somehow freezing it out.

Peck found Nick. "Mother's looped, right?"

Nick nodded. "She does this."

"Nicholas! She does this? She *does* this! What do you mean? For how long?"

"For a while now."

"What's a while?"

"I started noticing about four years ago."

Peck pushed his brother against a wall and tipped over a tray of wine glasses, which immediately made him feel shitty; he apologized and backed off.

"It's never violent or anything," Nick confessed now. "I mean, you know mother; she'd never ... act badly or whatever."

"Yeah. Yeah, I know," Peck said.

The following week, Peck made calls to Minnesota to a recovery hospital, whose good work he had heard about. It was hard for him to focus. He seemed to be carrying Victoria's body around with him since their moratorium or whatever it was had certainly ended. When he could break free from filming ten days later, he caught the shuttle to Boston and set brass to brass at his parents' house, knocking at the door at about seven that evening. His father received him, looking surprised. Peck entered and hung his overcoat in the front hall closet the way, as a child, he had seen his father do. They moved into the dining room, where his mother sat at her traditional end of the table, dishes and glasses still uncleared. She was smoking a cigarette and her face had the same glaze as puff pastry.

Dr. Peck inquired, "Well, to what do we owe this unexpected honor?"

"Are you getting a divorce," his mother asked, "so soon?"

Peck outlined his intentions. His mother rushed from the room crying. His father was furious. "How dare you!" he said.

"To dare is easy," Peck said. "Yes, I dare. It's only a beginning."

They argued. Dr. Peck demanded that Peck leave and threatened to call the police. Peck's mother could be heard in throes of tears upstairs, then padding unevenly down and plunging past them—Peck knew where. He could hear the click of the cabinet door, the movement of bottles and music of glasses. "We're dealing with this!" Dr. Peck informed him. "You have no concept ... no legal grounding."

"This is a top facility," Peck informed his father. "They're the best. I'll pay."

"You're an arrogant son of a bitch!" his father told him.

"Please, both of you, stop this!" Peck's mother hissed as she hurled herself into the room, tripped on the Tabriz, and fell.

"See what you've done?" Peck's father said, pointing.

"I want to go! Please, Arthur!" Peck's mother sobbed into the candelabra of flowers knotted into the rug.

Together they flew her to Minnesota. Nick was on call and couldn't make the trip. Mrs. Peck wore a blue suit and silk blouse, kidskin gloves, Ferragamo shoes. She had her hair done for the trip. On the flight, for the first time, Peck noticed that his father's hands housed a tremor. Every magazine his father tried to hold fluttered. Peck's mother pulled her gloves off, finger by finger, then drew them on again. Peck stopped counting the ritual at eighteen. She spoke little, only commenting on how nice everybody was: "Such a nice attendant, ... such a nice young man across the aisle, ... such a nice voice, the captain's."

They talked to the doctors and the nuns who ran the hospital. "I'm not Catholic. Will it matter?" Mrs. Peck asked. She was assured it would not matter.

"I feel like I'm the one being instructed. I feel like I'm the one being interviewed here," Dr. Peck objected at one point.

"Mrs. Peck's staying, you're not," Sister Loraine informed Dr. Peck shyly.

When they parted, Mrs. Peck held her son longer and more fiercely than he remembered her ever having held him. "Thank you!" she growled privately into his ear. She shook her husband's hand. They kissed each other's cheeks.

They hadn't eaten except for a powdered-egg omelette on the plane, and so Dr. Peck suggested they eat in Minneapolis. "Chinese?" he asked. Peck smiled. He grabbed his father and drew him in to a hug. "What? What are you doing?" his father wanted to know.

"You said something once," Peck confided, "and I remember it."

"What?"

"All we ask is that you try."

Back on Mott Street, on their third floor, there was dust and plaster everywhere. J.T. was in the middle of it. "Hey, buddy!" he greeted Peck. He had bought the apartment next door and was doubling their space as a wedding present. Victoria sat in it all, serenely situated on a futon, reading Rudolph Bultman. "Hi, sweetheart," she said. "Was it all right?"

Peck told her he was hopeful.

"Drunks are a problem!" J.T. said brutally. He was nothing if not frontal. Rolls of permatape hung from the curtain rods. "Listen, you two might want to get a hotel for a week or so," he suggested. Peck thought it a good suggestion. They packed bags and moved up to the Essex House.

"This is like a honeymoon," Victoria said. Peck wondered how she absorbed him like she did. It was like an eddy or tidal pool or something akin to a current or undertow, an undeniably physical attraction which drew him in. Where had she learned that? Was that something learnable, practiceable, like a golf shot?

"The air sounds different here ... in these different lights," she observed as they lay together in the otherwise dark room and smelled the faintly humid linen.

The air sounds different here? Peck thought. Where did she retrieve such a notion, one so intent and untranslatable? That another person could be so much of herself and yet so much of him made Peck shudder. He would never know her, he thought. He would never know her fully, and that would be their lifetime.

Still, of the present and in the moment, something was clearly imbalanced in the course of the planets. A month and a half back from Minnesota, filming the week's episode at the studio, Peck received a message to "call Jessica." It was a number in Brooklyn. "No last name?" Peck asked. "She didn't say," the assistant who had taken the call said.

Into the void, out of the void, Peck thought, *and the divination of secrets.* He took the risk, which was hardly a new kind of strategy for his life. Jessica, of course, was *Jessica.*

"Can I see you?" she asked, then "please?"

Peck thought he needed to *be visible, above-board* and arranged for a meeting during a break at the studio the next day. She wanted to know whether there might not possibly be somewhere more private. He said he didn't think so. "Anything you can say here and now?" he asked. She said no.

That evening, dissolved into Victoria, Peck considered mentioning he was having lunch the next day with an old girl friend. But his mind went turquoise ... and gold, and the thought went.

"I watch your program every week," Jessica said even before *How are you?* or *Good to see you.* "Every Thursday."

"Well, that's when it's on," Peck joked.

They went to a small Italian restaurant that featured Puccini on the jukebox. She looked as he remembered her, with the prettiness that intelligence etches, flushed with the thought of submitting to an emotion which might overwhelm her. Her clothes were less modest than herself. Peck said immediately that he was married, and Jessica drew silent. She shredded two napkins and hurried her wine. "You didn't send an announcement," she said, finally. Peck deferred, saying that he thought the wedding had been pretty much covered in the media.

"Oh, well, of course, the *media*," she snapped.

Peck wanted to tell her *Hey, you're the one who didn't answer my calls … remember?*

They picked at their antipasto. Jessica broke down in tears. She had married a man, Lewis Haseltine III, who was ten years older. He had an independent income and quasi-career as an opera singer, which took him on tour. She was discouraged from accompanying him. Lewis had a hyperactive child from a previous marriage. After three years of Jessica's questioning her own biology, he said he had forgotten to mention that he'd had a vasectomy and that one child was enough. Her house was lovely. She had charge accounts. She'd been writing, published some poetry. But she had psychosomatic cramps and unbearable longings. She thought about Peck constantly and about their confused times. It was imperative that he have an affair with her.

"Whoa," Peck said. "Wait a minute."

Jessica left for the ladies' room. When she came back, she said: "I don't think you understand. I don't think I can hang on."

"Jessica," Peck said, "you can't …"

She ripped off a corner of her place mat and scribbled on it.

She pushed the message at Peck: "There's the address where I'll be in Brooklyn for the next five days and the hours when no one else will be there ... to interrupt anything. Here's the number." She rose, snatched her coat, and left.

For the five days, Peck kept the scrap of paper in his pocket. He told himself it was a test, something like the Civil Defense announcement looping over and over again through his brain. He would get called to the phone at the studio. There would be someone there, but whoever it was would not speak. At Peck and Victoria's on Mott Street, the phone would ring. "Hello? ... Hello?" Peck would try, but there would only be the waiting silence. After five days, the calls stopped.

That week on his radio spot, Peck said: "Watch my hands, watch my hands!" He made the sound of flash powder, of spontaneously combusting smoke. "Good Lord!" Peck shouted into the radio mic: "What's this? ... a former lover? Where did *she* come from? *She* wasn't supposed to appear. It was supposed to be a first-born child!"

Victoria, who had heard the show, met him at the door. "How did you know?" she asked.

"How—"

"How did you know today on your radio show about the first-born child thing. I'm pregnant."

Peck encircled her and tears exploded—gushed up from his throat, poured from his eyes. "Oh my God!" He had never felt so blessed, so grateful.

The next day he was offered an hour television special. *Out of the void,* he kept saying to himself, *what's not supposed to happen happens ... or it doesn't ... or ...* He felt spun around, humbled and confused. He couldn't believe his life. His own performance was tricking him. The following week Kelson Kopf called. Paramount was offering a movie. Peck told Jack Gilson he needed a week off. Whatever the series needed to do, if they wanted him to continue, they needed to allow it.

He took Victoria on a cruise to Aruba. She'd traveled with him to Los Angeles on business. He'd performed at the Desert Inn in Las Vegas once and she'd come with him. They'd flown the previous summer to Santiago, Spain. Peck told her he needed to drift. He said he needed to float and not have thoughts for as long as possible. Victoria had her own secrets of how to enable that.

At the end of the week when they returned, the phone had stopped ringing. Peck was more in love with Victoria than seemed humanly possible. How did that happen? Where did more love come from? Was there a black box with mirrors somewhere? He found himself in tears at least twice a day that he, Peck, at thirty-three years of age, would be a father. He took the television special. He took the movie. He called his mother in Minnesota. She sounded alive and more connected than she had sounded in years.

Eight

P eck relished his life. He rejoiced. Busy as he was, he would sit with Victoria in their redoubled space while she explained Wittgenstein to him. If Peck caught the drift, Wittgenstein was a magician. In the *Tractatus* and in *Philosophical Investigations,* he made words, even whole ideas, appear and disappear. And Victoria was so delicate and elegant, even when she was pregnant, in the way she said words like *elucidations* and *criteria.* Her sentences were like Delft, her breath like fine glaze.

He never grew tired. Even weariness held its celebration. He flew regularly to Minnesota. He made new efforts with his father, and even though the elder Peck seemed, without his attending wife, increasingly autumnal and sere, the two groped toward a new father-and-son language.

When his shooting schedule permitted, Peck would sit in on Columbia lectures and seminars with his wife. He confessed that some of her professors might work harder on their performance. He felt most of them lacked any real sense of audience. He went on sprees with J.T., sometimes close at hand in town for evenings of jazz and too much whiskey, sometimes abroad for forty-eight hours in Zagreb or Dubrovnik. "I just feel like going to Croatia," J.T. would say; "How can you not go to a place named Croatia?"

Peck commissioned two new Russell songs for his hour special. He arranged dates between Russell and every impressionable single woman he could find, then provided solace when Russell would say: "It's no use. I blew it. It's never going to happen."

Russell increasingly hated his work. Though his fees rose and rose, he said most of his entertainment clients "didn't *entertain*, … they gave *hand jobs*." Peck considered hiring Russell to work for him, perhaps as personal manager, but knew Russell would see it as a judgment, and that it would hurt, so he rejected the notion.

Victoria moved into her fifth month. Peck asked about ultrasound. She said no. She said why. She said, "Do you need to know?" He said no, of course not, it was only a question. She moved into her sixth month and it seemed to Peck that she was incapable of further expansion. She moved into her seventh. Her eighth. Peck's excitement kept going off like a maverick security system. He did his hour-long television special three weeks before Victoria gave birth. He was a bit odd on the show. He was mystifying and confounding. He was constantly moving and throwing his arms out to the universe in an obvious gesture of rapture and speaking of "all this amazing invisibility!"

On the night the show was aired, in his ultimate trick—one nobody on the production staff or at the network was prepared for—whole pieces of the video disappeared. There were seconds and even close to a minute of blank screen, with only audio. The tape was whole; it was all there, there were no erasures. But somehow Peck had engineered making entire sequences disappear. In addition, there were inserts that appeared out of nowhere—audio inserts like Peck's voice under the blank screen saying "Where did I go? Where did the program go? This is wild!" And there were sudden video inserts of Peck appearing in a different costume in the middle of one of his comedy monologues, saying: "We're still trying to figure out where I disappeared to ... and how it happened." When the president of the network called Peck the next day, very possibly angry, and asked how he did it, Peck said simply that a magician never reveals his tricks.

It was fun. That was the whole idea. He was about to become a father and life was fun. His ratings were incredible. The most amazing part, though, happened after the special's airing. The vanished segments of the show appeared mysteriously in the middle of other shows, one even on another network. Under them was Peck's voice saying, "Whoops ... wrong show!" "Yikes, wrong network!" and "Sorry, I'm still learning this one."

Victoria and Peck were having *abalone lo mein* with her family when her water broke. Mr. Gow turned to Peck: "You do this?" he said. "This a joke? This your trick?"

In the cab, winding to New York University Hospital, Peck held his wife, he knew, as gently as he had ever held a woman. An hour later, he was gowned and masked with her in the delivery room. Her eyes were full and radiant and she seemed to float on the sea of herself like a muscled swimmer. *Out of the void,* he kept intoning to himself through tears. And then it happened ... It happened *out of the bloody, raging void. I can't believe it!*

They immediately decided to name them Leigh and Lee, the firstborn a female and the twin a male: Leigh Gow and Lee Nicholas Peck. Their father spun and danced like an untethered astronaut under the surgical lights. The space smelled dank and amniotic. Peck could taste iron on his teeth. He felt drugged. He felt like Chaplin or Harold Lloyd on a space probe. He wanted to lift Victoria with his two hands and hold her above his head and say: "Hey, world! Hey! This is my wife!"

Victoria produced milk from somewhere. It amazed Peck. Where in her dear fragility did all this milk come from? *Biology is magic,* Peck thought, not so much destiny. Lee and Leigh doubled their body weights. They squirmed, they stretched and scanned their eyes and reached limbs out to find worlds that made sounds and moved beyond them. They were breathtaking. They were fabulous.

Peck, given that he was Peck, thought to lay his claim, set his signature on Lee and Leigh's being of his life. One afternoon he took them from their tandem cribs such that, when Victoria looked in on them, it appeared that they had disappeared.

She screamed and shrieked and wailed. Peck immediately brought them back—strolled into the room with a twin cradled in each arm.

"What were you thinking?" Victoria demanded.

Peck felt ashamed. "I suppose I was thinking, I was hoping—"

"*Don't you ever, ever do that again,*" Victoria shrieked: "Ever … ever! These are *children!*"

"I know that."

"No props! No effects!"

Peck felt shabby and carnival. His vocation seemed cheap. He thought he'd never be able to atone for his insensitivity.

He made up a photo album of the twins and carried it to Minnesota to show his mother. When he got to her room, she wasn't there. No one on the staff had seen her all day. "Did you see her yesterday?" Peck asked. They weren't sure. "What about the day before that?" Her clothes were there, her hairbrushes, her facial cream, her *Book of Common Prayer*. It seemed his mother had suddenly disappeared. *Lord! Good Lord, where?*

Peck paced the corridors. He raged at one of the attending physicians and tried not to rage at the supervising nun. Nearly four hours after his arrival, he spotted his mother drifting along like some dust phantom at the far end of a hall. "Where have you been?" he asked her.

"I didn't know you were coming," she said.

Peck repeated his question. The deep breaths he found himself taking gave his head an anaesthetic buzz.

Mrs. Peck said she had needed to test herself. She left the grounds, she said, took a bus to Minneapolis, rented a room, and bought three bottles of Campari. She lined up the bottles on her bureau and had simply, for two days, lived with them. "There will be liquor when I get home," she said. "Your father won't just throw out that wonderful wine his patients give him. It's not going to simply vanish. That won't happen. I'm going to have to live with it all—every bottle, all within reach."

Peck drew her in as tightly as he dared. These days, she felt and looked so immaterial. He told her he was proud. He said she was strong.

"Oh, no," his mother said, "not strong—not me. Just realistic."

He showed her the Lee and Leigh album he had brought.

"Funny," his mother said.

"What do you mean?"

"Just *funny*. They don't *look* Chinese," his mother said.

At the Crestview Motel that evening during the six o'clock

news and sports report, a man appeared at Peck's door bearing a fourteen-inch lobster pizza. Peck hadn't placed a call, "but I'll take it," he said, and gave the man a twenty. He set the pizza on his bed and cracked a bottle of Campari and sat, squinting into the text of *Principia Mathematica* because it was a book Victoria loved. He had promised he would attempt to read it. *This man, this Wittgenstein simply isn't funny,* he thought.

When his room phone rang, Peck inventoried the list of possible callers: Victoria, his mother, father, Nicholas, or at the outside edge Kelson Kopf. Peck answered.

"Peck?" the voice asked. Peck's lungs filled with helium. It was *Jessica.* He could barely decode her intent through her viscous voice, filled with sobs. She had left her husband, she said. She had called Peck in New York, though without identifying herself, and had said it was critical she get in touch with him. "Your wife recognizes desperation," Jessica said.

Victoria had given Jessica her husband's information, after which Jessica had immediately flown to Minnesota.

"Where are you now?" Peck asked.

"I'm in the phone kiosk in the motel parking lot," she said. "I'm not going away. You have to see me."

"Okay," Peck said. He felt at the edge of a tornado. "Okay, I guess you've got me a bit cornered here."

She arrived at his door and exploded in. "I know! I know it's a cliché, and I hate it. I've always hated vulgar clichés. But Peck, would you hold me, please?" Then she was against him, clutching hard, wracked and miserable. Peck brought his hands around to her back, and it was as though they were dancing again.

"Would you like some lobster pizza?" he tried. "Or Campari, or both."

Jessica told him *just a minute* then made diminishing sounds like an engine with faulty compression running down.

When she felt quieted, they sat together on the bed, breaking crust between their teeth, filling the room with the smells of tomato paste and steamed cardboard. Jessica spilled her story. Lewis had become dismissive and cruel. He lived in a private life almost entirely, calling in from wherever that orbit might have been with the most insulting of stories and excuses. There would often be laughter in the background. She had obviously become his joke.

She sobbed again. She clung, getting lobster and lipstick and olive oil all over Peck's shirt. "Will those come out?" she asked of her design of stains. Peck flourished a hand over them. Nothing. "Sometimes it works," he said.

They talked into the middle of the night ... about what hadn't happened between them and why. They used hindsight and speculation and what their years had brought. Jessica used more psychological buzzwords than Peck, who drew a bit heavy on performance metaphors. They snuggled briefly. They kissed, once deeply; and then drew back with the chill of danger rippling their skin. "Oh my," Jessica said. "Yes, that's it for now, I'm afraid," Peck concurred. They talked some more, nearly until dawn. They invented the life they might have had. Peck said that, all in all, his life had been really quite astonishing. He felt grateful for it and would not betray it. Jessica said she understood. They agreed to stay close and call one another. She called a cab and left. In the muffled and frozen air, the cab pulling away, Jessica rolled down her window and Peck thought he heard her voice vanish into the air: *And now you're saying no to me.*

The movie Peck had signed on to co-starred J.T. Dennis. Paramount loved them as a team. The director, Leon Orchid, said: "It's like one of you is the juggler and the other is the balls." "I'm the balls," J.T. said. The script had two American correspondents covering a hostage situation in some exotic foreign country. Drafts of the film kept changing the locale from Egypt to Tibet, Peru, Kenya, and finally to the Greek island of Corfu. Leon Orchid, who weighed over three hundred pounds, couldn't decide where the food was best.

Using his star leverage, Peck finagled a small part for Russell, so his friend took a three-week vacation from his law practice. It was late June in Peck's thirty-sixth year when *Making Due* closed down for a summer of reruns. Peck hugged Leigh and Lee and their mother, then with his two best friends climbed aboard a United jet at La Guardia for Corfu.

The shoot was to last six wonderful weeks. Peck missed his family and ran up astronomical cell phone bills. Still, if males have fantasies about close and giddy capers with other males, Peck got to live them. He and J.T. were given some license with the script, and what elaborations were missing from the film, they continued in their off-time. There were pranks. There were inspired and creative sabotages. Leon Orchid, who had some bastard lineage to Stanislavsky, saw himself as the genius orchestrating a brilliant "sense-memory chemistry" between two gifted madmen. "It's like what would have happened," he beamed, "if Fields and Keaton had been a team."

It was, in fact, a strange and magical mix. Every day, J.T. tore at the project's fabric with his teeth. Then Peck somehow repaired it, making it seamless. Russell was like the boy Peck had first met as a freshman at Bard. The entire world had become some sort of lute for Russell to pluck. In one scene, unannounced, he strolled through a café, composing as he picked out a haunting song on a tamboura. "Brilliant! Keep it!" Leon Orchid boomed.

They had mopeds and wound out to the beach at Paleokastritsa whenever time allowed. They dove from the cliffs, they swam into the caves. Peck reported it all by cell phone to Victoria. "Come," he pleaded: "Come here! Fly here and bring the twins!" J.T. fell in love with a Greek girl named Kalli, discovered in a beach taverna. She wore flowers in her hair, and Peck saw trouble coming. J.T. in love was like a hurricane forming miles out at sea: you knew it would just be a matter of time before trees were uprooted, entire harbors overturned.

There were red flags from Russell, as well, and had Peck been more alert to his friend's manic contagion, he would have taken more precautions. As it was, Russell drank less than Peck had expected, but the times he did drink were so all-out, unbounded, they were fairly worrisome. If Russell had wanted to be Peck at one time, he now wanted to be J.T. Peck's one friend fell in love with the beflowered Kalli, as Russell simultaneously fell in love with Kalli's friend, Celia. Both girls' parents were opposed to their daughters seeing the American actors. Charmed and mischievous, the girls defied tradition and walked the topless beaches, saucy, breasts pert, hands in the hands of their new and quite dangerous lovers. The more settled husband and father in Peck saw trouble under it all.

And of course, trouble soon came. Kalli was already promised in an arranged marriage to a young man named Aristo. J.T. knew this because Kalli had pointed out Aristo to him. At dusk one day, J.T. spotted Aristo and Kalli having *retsina* and *calamari* at a café in the Old Harbor. Both sets of parents were there. J.T. felt flames in his brain, and they leapt, uncontained, from his eyes. He seized an eggplant from an open-market cart, threw down too many drachmas, and punched a hole in the vegetable with a ballpoint pen.

"What are you doing?" Peck asked.

J.T. said nothing. He took on heat like the core of a nuclear reactor. He bought a bottle of *ouzo*, poured it into the eggplant, created a fuse from newspaper, and hurled his bomb, purple and pulpy, toward the café.

Rage pumps adrenalin. The eggplant sailed nearly fifty yards over the café tables and landed in a yacht, where it exploded, peppering the sails with dark rind and tiny seeds. Fortunately, no one was aboard, but the Corfu harbor police were soon on J.T. like deer to a salt block, weapons drawn.

Kalli, seeing what was happening, shrieked hysterically in high-decibel Greek. J.T. barked: "Am I being arrested because I *missed*? I'm an *actor*, not a *quarterback*. Was it a bad performance?"

Peck tried to mediate, but his friend was taken off to the government courthouse on the hill.

J.T. returned within hours to the set at who knows what cost to Paramount. But all his remaining days' takes were inspired. "Grape growers!" he grumbled under his breath. "Boat builders! ... Who needs 'em? Assholes!" "I hate women!" he boomed at one point: "I hate all women!" It was in the middle of a love scene. "Yes! Yes! Keep it!" Leon Orchid shouted. He seemed thrilled.

The next caper involved J.T. renting a café on Theotoki Street for three nights. He retained the kitchen staff and waiters, but the challenge to his friends was to "show 'em how it's done." The three sang country & western music, did comedy sketches with two Greek interpreters, and Peck did some magic. The *ouzo* was liberal, the place overflowed with locals and tourists. They ran beyond all appointed hours, each night, until the police arrived. "The Corfu curfew!" J.T. barked when the police closed them down.

On a Friday dawn, the three stood on top of some rugged rocks and surveyed the Aegean. "Okay, we're not ancients," Peck observed, "but we've had our time. We've courted some legends of our own." They all agreed.

Russell's shooting was done and he was about to head home. At the café, he got more desperately drunk each successive night and sang better in some ways, worse in others, and improvised with amazing inspiration on his guitar. Peck got chills. He got chills for what Russell might have been and for what the desperation signaled. The last night, when the lights on their short-term café went dark, Russell went on a brutal crying jag. Peck noticed at the airport, as Russell boarded Olympic Airlines, that he looked like someone from beyond the grave.

Peck called Victoria: "Please, hon: call Russell and invite him up for dinner. Get him to talk. Get him to tell some stories. Make sure he comes." All the signals were there.

The filming wrapped up. Leon Orchid believed a whole anthology had been launched and talked about the possibility of sequels: DETAILS AT TEN: PARIS, ... DETAILS AT TEN: KYOTO, ... DETAILS AT TEN: PUERTO VALLARTA. "Just think of the food," he said.

J.T. and Peck took an extra day to unwind at a nude beach. They tossed a football. They drank beer. "I'd like to get into a good mixed volleyball game," J.T. said, but they didn't find one. J.T. felt restless. Peck felt subdued. He missed his wife, he missed his children.

In late August, home only three weeks, Making Due started up for its fifth and final season. Life resumed. The twins were walking, even talking. Victoria finally received her degree. She speculated about finding a job. The two weighed a bigger apartment. Peck spoke to the Gows. He wanted to finance a Low's East at an available location on upper Amsterdam. The Gows were hesitant.

Peck was shooting segments daily. His mother graduated from the hospital and had shown off her diploma in sobriety. She was back with Dr. Peck in Boston and seemed relieved and cheerier when she and Peck chatted. Nick and Lanie had their third child. Nick was in a thriving radiology clinic and was teaching part-time at Boston University Medical School.

Peck also did his weekly "Radio Magic" spot. He read scripts for new movies. He held talks about a second television special. He turned thirty-eight. Jessica wrote, saying she had entered law school at UCLA. "It's what I should have done in the first place," she said. She gave her new phone and address. "I'm okay," she wrote; "I'm calmer." Peck didn't pick up that feeling in her letter; he couldn't tell if *calmer* were actually true.

DETAILS AT TEN came out and was a hit. Peck did interviews. Magazines featured him. He and Victoria did a round of parties, east and west coasts, that seemed like fantasy. J.T. admired what he called "class" when he met people like Paul Newman, Henry Fonda, Norman Mailer, Beverly Southerland, Frank Stella. He tried drawing Peck and Victoria into a social circle, but it all seemed strange to Peck, like an Italian movie. Mostly he begged off. "You're hurting my feelings, you realize that," J.T. would say.

Through all of this, Peck tried to stay in close contact with Russell. It wasn't easy because Russell was either very up or very down—highs and lows. One night, at two, he called and said: "I'm getting married. I'm getting married! Whoops, sorry I woke you up. I'll call tomorrow." When three days passed and he didn't call, Peck telephoned him. Russell's voice seemed undriven by any muscle. "It was nothing," he said. "It was just a thing I believed, I thought … It was an idea that didn't go anywhere, a thought I had."

"You all right?" Peck asked.

"I'm fine," Russell replied. "No, I'm fine. Hey, no problem."

Then, when DETAILS AT TEN was nominated for an audience award, Russell was flying again. He did a round of parties. He encountered women who wouldn't let go of his suit jacket. Peck saw more violent drinking. He sat through additional crying jags.

Before long, the movie hype faded and the film declined in box office sales. Other movies took its place, other people, other parties. In April, Peck got a call one morning from a partner at Russell's firm. This time the gun had been real and he'd put it in his mouth and fired. The funeral was to be in two days.

Peck flew to Philadephia and spoke. For the first time in his life, in front of people, he was shaking. "Russell is gone," he said. "What's supposed to happen doesn't. What's not supposed to happen does, that's all the sense I can make of it." For the last nearly ten years, everything had been *appearing* out of the blue. Now his dearest friend had *disappeared.* "Where did he go? I'm a magician. I should be able to answer that." Peck wept openly. "I confess I can't answer that," he said. It felt like the very words he spoke gave up their substance and floated *into the void, and then where?*

Nine

After Russell's death, Peck just wanted to love everyone he
loved. He held Victoria in ways he had never held her
and did so through entire nights. He sat absolutely still and
watched his children as though they were new planets in a
just-discovered galaxy. He wrote a long and rambling letter to
Jessica, talking about "the things that last and why they're important." He flew to Boston, where he was *uncle* and *brother*,
and loved that. "Tell me everything you can about your life and
about your work," he asked Nicholas.

"Hey man, what's going on with you?" Nicholas wondered.

His parents, though, remained a curious couple, Peck
thought. His mother was sober and the two lived in their old
house, their children gone, at ages sixty-three and sixty-six.
Peck wondered, in part, who they were. It was as though he
were in his dormer again, looking out, down, and through his
window into some other house, across air, across dividing
hedges, to watch a pair of people do what was called *living*. It
was mysterious and affecting. They seemed like nice enough

people, decent and industrious—still, they were not the parents he'd grown up with.

When *Making Due* ended, there were farewell parties. Jack Gilson cried and gave speeches, using words like "fellowship" and "community" more than a person ought to. Victoria came to most of the events. When she didn't, Peck and J.T. found some corner and yammered, and then walked the streets, casting back, casting forward, and being philosophical. DETAILS AT TEN: WARSAW was already cooking, although both Peck and J.T. thought the script was terrible. J.T. was in love again, this time with an Australian archeology student who was ten years younger. "I'm behaving myself, I swear" he said. "It's a promise, Pecker. I'm taking deep breaths and behaving myself."

He had just rolled over a cooperative in Chelsea for a profit of $170,000. "Five weeks!" he said. "I rebuilt three fireplaces."

Peck did a week in Las Vegas at Caesar's Palace and brought the family. He also sent airline tickets to his parents and to the Nicholas Pecks. The senior Dr. Peck said Las Vegas wasn't a place he cared to visit, and the junior doctor, although he considered sending Lanie and the kids, said there was no way he could break free. Ultimately he thanked his brother and backed out. Still, the immediate Pecks enjoyed their vacation. Lee and Leigh were four years old now and took swimming and tennis lessons. Victoria lay out poolside to read a biography of Marie Curie. Twice they sailed on Lake Mead. Victoria said it felt like something was pinching the inside of her head. Peck assumed it was just the sun.

The family flourished. They moved to Bedford, New York,

to a restored farmhouse. "Where are the animals?" Lee asked, echoed by Leigh. Their father soon produced sheep, one by one, from a lacquered box set out in the family room. He produced ducks at his fingertips. Lee and Leigh squealed. Victoria told Peck he shouldn't act in his home. Homes weren't for illusion. They were for family, for reality. He thought she had a point.

When Peck walked the property and the country roads, often he would think about how much like Annandale it was, and time would slip into a soluble sweet collapse, and he would think of Bard and, of course, Russell. Could he have been Russell? Under slightly different circumstances, could Russell have been him? Where were any of those thresholds? What were the critical points? He was an adult now: Jesus! He was nearly forty. And Russell was gone. Where was Leslie Fay? Where was Antony Foley?

Antony Foley was, in fact, to reappear, but not immediately. In the meantime, Peck had fulfilled his youthful threat to his father to become a celebrity. His engine was always running, and it was fueled by surprise. What he most loved and thrived on, and offered in a way no one else offered, was the unexpected. He made America smile. He made people wonder. He did a comedy album and tape based on his "Radio Magic" show that was so popular it generated three other albums.

He did two more DETAILS AT TEN in LENINGRAD and HAITI. During the LENINGRAD shoot, J.T. was in love with a painter named Estelle Foote. At the time of the HAITI production, it was a systems analyst named Robyn Robin. Always, adjacent structures were in jeopardy when J.T. was in love— walls, windows, wicker furniture.

Peck began hosting a weekly network variety show called

Watch Closely! on which, from time to time, he pulled off feats which were destined to become legendary. On one installment, he switched the Atlantic and Pacific oceans. The television camera framed surf breaking on cliffs, which Peck identified as Malibu. The next sequence showed surf breaking on sand announced to be Cape Ann. Then Peck mumbled magic words, reprieved the surf on the rocks, and told Cape Ann to become Malibu. Select witnesses on both coasts swore, though it happened only briefly, the switch had actually taken place.

Another time, during a live presidential news conference, the president's words came out in the voice of a famous cartoon duck. Another feat, one which would bring Peck to page one of every world newspaper, involved the Cheops pyramid. Somehow, for a half-hour period, long enough for a few people to arrive and photograph it, the pyramid disappeared from the west bank of the Nile and arrived in an alfalfa field outside O'Neill, Nebraska. The Egyptians were irate. The Governor of Nebraska issued an apology. Peck secured a place in history and future close surveillance by both the CIA and the FBI. There was considerable pressure on him, which he resisted, to issue a statement saying it had been only a trick, an illusion.

Victoria took a job in a blood laboratory. It made her happy. She taught Peck everything she knew about titration. She periodically noted what she had called the *pinching in her head*. She'd ask Peck to massage the very top of her scalp and told him it went away with the massage. Lee and Leigh entered pre-school. They entered school. They were soon approaching junior high. Lee excelled in music, Leigh in art, and both maintained an interest in tennis. Returning from a family trip to St. Croix one August, the Pecks discovered that J.T. had converted their barn into indoor tennis courts.

"I'm getting married," he said. "This is serious. Next month. Her name is Punch, Punch Alcott." It turned out she was a heavy equipment operator and drop-out from Vassar and was more incendiary in temper and passions than J.T. He stood in delighted awe when she pushed him off his chair at a cocktail lounge for calling the waitress "darlin'," an incident he loved retelling. "She's a killer," he said. "A killer!"

Peck liked Punch, but Victoria was cautious around her. They knew the match would either be sublime or lethally messy. Of course, time would prove them right.

He wrote Jessica, even saw her occasionally when he was in Los Angeles. She'd finished law school near the top of her class and had gone to work for a firm that specialized in ocean disputes and the atmosphere. "So, you're doing, I'm sorry ... what?" Peck asked at Paramount during a lunch with her one day: "You're chasing ambulances through ... I'm sorry, I need to get this straight, where? The Great Barrier Reef and the Milky Way, did you say?"

Jessica spoke with him about a new man in her life. Peck could never get his name sequence settled—Warren Jason or Jason Warren or something or other. She claimed he was wonderful and charming. Still, she'd begun seeing the signal lights of old traffic patterns and wasn't entirely sure. "Besides," she said, "if I marry him, then when you're free, I won't be available." Peck felt the hair on his spine tighten but wasn't sure why.

Peck's parents aged. Dr. Peck talked about retirement, saying how hard it was to keep precise histories. His mother said, "I'm glad I stopped being a drunk, but I'm not as happy." One visiting weekend, Lanie pulled Peck aside from Nicholas and broke down. "I have to tell you," she said, "I'm having an affair and may leave Nick."

"You're—"

"Having an affair."

"Right. I *heard* you," Peck said.

"I just felt you needed to—"

"I needed to ..."

Lanie pressed her fingertips against her chest.

"I needed to ... what? What's my role here, exactly, do you think?" Peck asked. "Who *am* I in this? What did you imagine my assignment would be?"

"I don't know," Lanie said; "I just—I don't know, I guess I just had to *speak* about it."

Peck yanked Nick aside and told him they were going to go on a trip to Idaho to do some stream fishing. Standing on the banks of the Salmon, Nick said: "You're a bully, you know? You kidnap me for something I don't have any aptitude for, just so you can laugh at me. I don't know anything about this shit!" He smiled. A monster trout struck his fly.

"Your marriage is in trouble," Peck said, once they'd coaxed the rainbow into a net. "Are you tracking at all with that or not?"

"I know," Nick said, and the two brothers hugged, waders to waders, in the current of the Salmon.

Nick tried to cut back his clinic hours and professional travel. He instigated options for counseling. He took Lanie to Hawaii. For a year, a turnabout looked possible; but then, whatever injury there was in Lanie, whatever her restlessness, it broke loose again. She packed. She filed. There was a gentle-faced cabinetmaker in the wings, five years younger, who had shoulder-length sandy hair. She gave Nick custody of

Willie and Willie's brother and sister. The older Pecks went from worn to spiritless at the news. "Everything's slipping away," Peck observed. "Everything's going up the universe's sleeve. It's all phantom and thin air." Nick seemed to be walking with a limp after the breakup. His posture became stiff.

Victoria's mother, Mrs. Gow, got badly burned when a wok-full of oil went up one night at Low's. It unraveled Victoria. She was an only child, and she left the Bedford farm to go and live with her parents and work again in the restaurant until Mrs. Gow regained her strength.

Peck walked the property alone. He paced the house. He hired a nanny, then let her go. She was a stranger. He looked at his children and realized they were at the age he'd been when his father had brought the first magic home. It seemed a ghostly truth, uncanny. What might he—as a father who sometimes wasn't at home for a month—give *them*? What might he inadvertently or on impulse bring home that might change their lives?

He thought about telescopes. He thought about fish for the pond, but it was winter. He thought Leigh might enjoy a loom, Lee a harpsichord.

He missed his wife. Peck was in an in-between period with his various projects, and without any demands, time seemed to float like a dreamy canopy above a marriage bed. When he saw his wife in New York, she seemed taut and anxious. There were tiny knots in the sweet flesh at her temples. She snapped often when he spoke. Mrs. Gow's skin had healed but was spotted. "I can't leave until the spots go," Victoria said. Peck wanted to ask Mrs. Gow whether her daughter seemed different to her, but he didn't command sufficient Chinese.

He took the twins to Bermuda. He took them to Disneyland. Victoria said she couldn't come. Peck knew there was more happening than met the eye. Such things were second-nature to him, he knew how to spot them. Victoria finally confessed that the *pinching* she had begun feeling had never left; she lived with a knife-stick of pain. Peck hurried her in for scans and x-rays. Her parietal lobe had an enlarging tumor. Could it be removed? Yes, but the procedure wasn't sure-fire. Peck walked the streets of Manhattan the entire night. He thought of getting very drunk but didn't. He was forty-two years old. He was famous. He was happy. He was a man who embraced all the visible and invisible world, who cherished his good fortune and was grateful. So, what now ... where? What direction? He went back to St. Vincent's and sat until Victoria woke. They reviewed the facts as presented and made choices. Certainly, they couldn't let the tumor flourish.

Peck spoke to the twins. "Your mother—" he said, searching for the line between immense, protective love and honesty.

"Will she die?" Lee asked.

"If she does, Daddy can make her alive again," Leigh said.

Peck tried to explain that there were certain events, certain acts—and he was very sorry—but they lay beyond him.

All current projects were cancelled. Nick, who was clearly putting on weight, flew down from Boston and made a sweet nuisance of himself, double-checking the scans. "I wish I could say otherwise, but these people are on top of it," he finally said.

Peck thanked his brother for wanting the facts overturned and for trying to look for another option. Peck wanted to be sure that Victoria felt as little pain as possible. The idea of her hurting, of her brain in combat, twisted him unmercifully. The operation was scheduled and the tumor removed. It was benign, but the chief surgeon, a man named Kalispell, said that even non-malignant … it had left its signature.

"Jesus, what does that mean!" Peck demanded, then apologized.

Kalispell told Peck Victoria was in a coma. There had been damage. He used another phrase which infuriated Peck, saying that "the circuitry was delicate." *Where did people learn to talk like this?* Peck steamed.

"What I want to know is if she'll *live*," he said. "Is she going to *live*?" He could never remember feeling such exploding pain and rage.

"There has been, and will continue to be, considerable swelling," he was told.

It flared into Peck's mind that if J.T. were here, he would have simply laid this guy out. He would have spread him onto the bloody wall.

Peck thanked Kalispell and walked off. He sat in Victoria's room. He made a single chrysanthemum appear and disappear above her bed at least two hundred times amid the sound of machines and the smell of fluids. Nothing fluttered when he brushed against her face or at the backs of her hands, places where, Peck had learned, the more durable and sure of her responses dwelled. *When the trick is over and has failed,* Peck remembered writing, *without announcement, it sometimes works … except this time,* he thought, *except no, not this time.*

Perhaps he was just weary. Perhaps he was discouraged. Perhaps his ordinary fierce intuition wasn't acute. He called Bedford and spoke with Mrs. Reese, the housekeeper. "Tell Lee and Leigh she's resting," he said. "Tell them she looks quiet and peaceful." Mrs. Reese said a man named Antony Foley had called and left a number for Peck to call him. Peck thanked her and wrote the number on the cuff of his shirt. *Unbelievable,* he thought. *Unbelievable!* What timing. REFENGE indeed!

Victoria died three days later. The services were private: the elder Pecks, the Gows, Nick and his three, J.T. and Punch, and of course, Peck, Lee, and Leigh. Jessica sent a telegram and flowers. Peck quoted Albert Einstein, whose words, he said, reflected the spirit of Victoria's sensibility and life. "I want to know how God created this world," he recited, trembling. "I am not interested in this or that phenomenon, in the spectrum of this or that element. I want to know His thoughts. The rest are details."

"No tricks?" Dr. Peck asked his son at graveside, following the internment.

Peck felt he lacked adequate life in his body to respond, even in anger.

"That was insensitive," his father said. "I don't know why I said it. I'm sorry."

Peck had never felt more like an observer. His father seemed, at least at the moment, like weather, like some random phenomenon.

Five days later his mother's life was swept to sea in a brutal coronary. Peck rushed home. In the dusk hours of the night before the funeral, family friends gathered. His mother's favorite wines were served with chilled lobster from Mosher's Fish Market and egg rolls and fantail shrimp from Joyce Chen's. It was a last embrace, a remembering and celebration.

Near the end of the gathering, Peck cornered his father and asked if he could please see his mother's heart.

His father stepped away, eyes lit like Sterno cans, his jaw seemingly dislocated.

Peck pursued. "The point is, you're a doctor. You can do that—open her up. You told me you did surgery in the war in

North Africa. I want to see her heart. It's important."

Dr. Peck looked on the verge of tears, then grew angry. "You're a selfish and deranged person!" he said to Peck and strode away.

Peck pressed Nicholas, who wrinkled his brow to show puzzlement and displeasure. But when Nicholas squeezed his upper lip between his thumb and forefinger, Peck saw an opening. "Do it!" he urged and heard Nicholas suck breath in. "Do it, Nicholas! For me, for us. She had the most amazing heart, don't you think? You *know* it was! It was amazing and rare. I want to see it. It won't take long. How long could it take? I can get us into the mortuary. I can get us through any wall, open anything. We'll be in and out. You do the surgery, ten minutes. *I'll* do the surgery if I have to. Just bring the stuff; bring your kit."

"My *kit*?"

"Tools, equipment, instruments, paraphernalia."

"*I'll* do the surgery."

That night after midnight, both brothers stood over their mother's body in the O'Driscoll Mortuary. "Who's going to undress her?" Nicholas asked.

Neither wanted to, so they finally agreed to do the undressing together. Each pulled on surgical gloves. Nicholas opened their mother gently, gently, folding away all that was necessary. He extended his gloved hands. "I feel like you," he said, "like it must feel when you're on stage doing magic."

Their mother's heart lay like a tearful pillow before them.

"All that goodness!" Peck managed in a voice that was reverent, hushed.

"So much," Nicholas said.

"It looks like there's light coming from it," Peck observed.

"There possibly is," Nicholas said. "What do *we* know? Why not?"

Peck slipped his hands under his mother's heart. It seemed weightless.

"Levitate it ... float it," Nicholas urged. And for a brief moment, both brothers felt that's what happened, what was done that evening in the mortuary.

Despite Peck's bothersome rambling the night before, his father asked if he would speak that morning at his mother's service. "You do well in public," he said. "You can be stupid, like you were yesterday. But in public, you change. You're good on stage."

Peck considered all the cruel possible responses, but chose none; rather, he agreed. In the Congregational church hours later, he rose to his feet when cued and spoke tremulously of the radiance of his mother. He spoke in tears of her heart. He spoke of the courage she'd shown surrounding her time in Minnesota. He told the Campari story. It occurred, in the telling, that his father might be upset and feel publicly compromised or shamed. But Peck felt the story was about his mother and that it framed her. It said she was a woman unlike others, kind and strong.

Nick thanked Peck for his words. Dr. Peck offered no comment. When Peck looked at his father—at the family home afterward amid the gathered doctors and doctors' wives—his father's lengthening face looked like it was webbed with a thousand hairline cracks that might, at any moment, give way, and it occurred to Peck how close to dust his father was.

It was a time of rites and ceremonies. Four days after Peck's mother's funeral, he stood handing J.T. a ring. "Do you, J.T. Dennis, take this woman ... Punch Alcott? ..." the empowered justice asked, voice echoing through a huge cinder-block garage J.T. had rented for the event. The announcements read: *You Are Invited to a Valentine's Day Massacre.*

The decor and dress were 1920s Chicago. It looked like a road company of *Guys & Dolls*. It featured bathtub gin and caviar. Peck's moment was to line up J.T. and Punch against the wall and spray them with a gun that fired confetti and rice. Peck wasn't up to it, really; he didn't feel celebratory and festive. Still, he was happy for his friend, and he could see his friend was genuinely happy. Peck conceded that Punch was something new for J.T. He had never fallen for a woman anything like her.

"You think this lug and I can make it?" Punch asked.

"I'm putting my prediction in a time capsule," Peck said.

It wasn't easy for Peck and his kids, reduced to three, but they managed. Peck stayed close. He tried to show love, if possible, enough for two people, and to be funny, strong, wise, tender. He read them David Hume and bought them chemistry sets. He taught them how to drive a stick shift, found them Chessmaster, spent hours running and re-running films of Buster Keaton, Harold Lloyd, and Charlie Chaplin. He tape recorded the sounds of Lee and Leigh's laughter.

Still, despite his focus on home—on trying to make and give love for both himself and the absent Victoria—he grew restless. His fingers moved as if knitting. He had trouble with sleep. The muscles at the back of his neck jumped and shifted and he developed a tic in his left eye. Home was lovely. Home was necessary and humbling and dear. But he needed to work. Work was in his shoulders, it was in his hands, it ran the length of his spine, gathered like saliva inside his mouth, and lit like birthday candles in the globes of his eyes.

So Peck re-engaged himself, let it be known that he was

again available. "Be selective. Just tell a few people," Peck told Kelson Kopf. A sea of *would you*s and *could you*s flooded in. Within a week, he'd settled on another sequel to DETAILS AT TEN—this one, *finally!* Leon Orchid said, in Paris.

Peck rehired the nanny he had hired and let go two years before, a Finnish woman named Sigre, who was blond and plump and cherry-cheeked. She was also old enough that her presence in Peck's house wouldn't confuse him. Sigre was his ersatz mother. She was the grey-blond Professor Nielsen, who he'd had for "Intro to Psych" at Bard; she was the Russian woman pulling puff pastries from the oven in the bakery he'd visited … somewhere, he couldn't remember.

So he packed for Orly—ransacking his closet in the process, smelling each and every shirt for the scent of Victoria, an inventory of sleeves and cuffs and collars that were sweet and crazed and charged with memory. Any shirts that smelled of unhappiness, he threw away into a green five-gallon garbage bag. And then …

And then, three years after the fact, he found a dress shirt squeezed in among the others with a phone number on its cuff: 201-575-0996. Under the number, Peck saw he'd written RE-FENGE. The 201 area code was New Jersey. Instinct warned Peck. Still, he felt compelled to call. The line rang four, five, six times, then as Peck thought he'd hang up, a voice, clearing itself three times before its *hello* and sounding rough and reptilian, answered. The voice sounded familiar and unfamiliar. The criminality was there but not as eager—more sad, distrustful, and tired.

The first words Antony Foley said after their *hellos* were, "Isn't it crazy … what we do when we're kids?"

As much as Peck could determine, Antony had become his

father's child making a living *closing deals*. He lived in the town of Nesco, with *affiliations*, he said, in Philadelphia and Atlantic City. He'd followed Peck's career with "pride and interest," and although his initial call had been "just to say hello," now, today, because they were friends, Antony wanted to "apprise" him of an opportunity which involved land along Mississippi's gulf coast. It was undeveloped, and Antony had "inside information" of plans underway to convert it into "a major retirement community along the lines of Sun City in Arizona." Peck could get in on "a major piece of the action" if he wanted for only a hundred thousand.

None of the underlying criminal inflections in Antony Foley's voice had dissolved over time. They made Peck smile. Nostalgia has a wicked curiosity, and they agreed to meet. Antony knew a "sensational" restaurant just off the pike near Woodbridge. "Friends of friends," he said. "Wonderful people. Greeks."

The morning of the day Peck was scheduled to meet Antony, Jessica called. How was Peck doing? She'd seen his *PARIS* sequel and it was the best yet. He was strong, she knew, and it had been some time, but was he okay and were things falling in place? Was he holding on? She was a partner in her firm now and was treating herself with a trip east, staying at the Essex House; might they see one another?

Peck felt like, at the age of forty-five, he was in high school again. Should he cancel Antony Foley and make a date with Jessica? What he suggested was that she take the train up to Bedford the next day to see where he lived, meet his children, spend the night. "Do you think I should?" Jessica asked. "Why not?" Peck said.

Peck knew clothes, and Antony was wearing a knock-off, look-alike Georgio Armani suit. It looked mismatched on his half-meaty, half-bony frame. The place was a roadhouse called *Boone's*. The waiter recommended a lambchop and fried oyster combo. Antony's greeting felt like padded teeth clamping Peck's hand. "You look exactly the same," Antony said, "exactly, exactly the same!" and Peck wondered *exactly the same as what?*

Peck listened. Antony jived and pushed and kept excusing himself to the men's room. His nose ran. He made three dreadful jokes at the expense of the elderly before Peck intervened. "So, your folks still hanging in there?" Antony asked. Peck asked to see pictures of the land, a map, perhaps, indicating where it might be found. "You don't believe me?" Antony said. He laughed. "Of course, I'll show you pictures," he said, and produced some scenes that were so generic, they could have been in Belgium. "It's a fabulous opportunity," Antony said. "Thing is, there's a deadline. It's now or never."

Peck withdrew his checkbook. Antony's eyes made a *sound,* they moved so deliberately to the rims of their sockets. Peck wrote. Antony kept saying, "You won't be sorry." When Peck handed him the check, Antony's face collapsed. "It's for five hundred dollars," he said. Peck apologized that he had no interest in the land. It seemed clearly bogus, he said, but he could see Antony had some needs in his life, needs which perhaps the money would help.

Antony pulled a small handgun and leveled it at Peck. Nearby patrons screamed. Antony pocketed the gun. "Hey, this guy and I are old friends," he said. "He knows me. I'm kidding. It's a joke." Hushed, he leaned in over his linguini with clam sauce and said, "Know this, boyo: your life means shit now. No one makes me look foolish."

Driving home to Bedford in a weave with imagined moments with Jessica, it occurred to Peck that he had not been prudent. He met Jessica at the Bedford station and was floored. Her essentially plain and intelligent beauty had been transformed into a fashionable and alluring look. He wanted to ask her, *How did you do that?* but realized it would be rude. When they embraced, she felt softer, smelled exotic. "Success does well by you," Peck tried.

"I have a different relationship with myself, I think, these days," Jessica said.

Peck believed her.

They drove and chatted. The March fields still had some shroud of winter. Again, Jessica asked how Peck was doing. Was there still pain? Was there anger? Did he sense a different relationship with the twins? Peck tried to respond, saying: "You're good to ask all these things."

They built a fire. The twins weren't home from school yet. Peck told his Antony Foley story. Jessica warned him that Antony "was always a creepy and violent guy." Peck teased her. He said that *back then* she would not have known *creepy* or *violent* from Adam. She said that perhaps their ongoing problem was that he continued to underestimate her.

"Ongoing?" Peck said and laughed.

"Ongoing," she repeated.

Peck threw his hands up in a gesture of surrender. Jessica leaned in to him and they kissed. When they drew back from the kiss, neither had the presence of words. Just then the back screen door slapped closed. Leigh and Lee were home.

Peck made introductions. Leigh said she had junior symphony practice, could she borrow the Subaru. Lee was going to change and practice tennis shots in the barn.

"They're both so … adult," Jessica said after they'd left. "I'd imagined them younger."

"I know, I imagine them younger, too," Peck said, "forever. Forever fourteen, you know. But—"

"Peck, what I meant was that they're beautiful," Jessica said, "and seem so content—wise and almost mature."

Peck felt pride. "I believe they are," he said. "Either or all—both."

Jessica asked Peck if he dated. Had he met anyone in the time since Victoria? "These are awkward questions," she said, "but I wanted to ask them."

Peck asked, "What about you?"

Jessica ran both her self-appraisal and recent history. She said: "It's funny, the more I succeed professionally, the more I know I could now personally feel comfortable, but the less important it all is." She asked Peck whether what she'd said made any sense.

He looked at her without answering. *Clearly* it made sense. She looked so beautiful. He leaned in to kiss her, but she drew back.

"This is a familiar scene," Peck said.

"Somehow, a Thursday afternoon with one of your children home doesn't feel quite right," she suggested. He agreed. "And you?" she asked, getting back to her original question.

"At best, escapades," Peck said.

"And is that, right now, how you'd have it? Is that fine?"

"It's sufficient," Peck said.

"Escapades aren't bad. They don't have to be," Jessica observed.

"I don't know. They feel a little bit illusory to me," Peck said.

"Well," Jessica said and smiled. "What's for supper?"

The answer was veal piccata and caesar salad. Peck directed. Leigh, who had the gift, cooked and everyone else chipped in. They shared a fumé blanc. "Tell us what our father was like in high school," Lee asked, and Jessica told any number of Peck stories, which left both twins rapt and disbelieving and gleeful. "I knew it! I *knew* it!" one of them would say and then the other would chime in with agreement. It was a sweet evening and felt familial again, without reserve, the way it had not been now for several years. Peck felt his emotions rising from somewhere in his chest to behind his ears to some frontal system threatening his eyes. He pulled himself in with whatever reserve he could summon.

That night after everyone had turned in and sleep was evasive, Peck found himself in only pajama bottoms at the foot of the guest room bed, watching Jessica sleep. How had she taken on such beauty? What was he thinking, imagining, by being there? What event was his breath being held in anticipation of?

She stirred, then woke. "Peck," she said. Her voice was husky from sleep. "No," she said, from the same slow and rounded place. "No. It's why I came, but no."

Peck left. He stood in the upstairs hall of his own house. He felt hurt. He felt solitary. He felt angry. He called Jessica a *bitch* under his breath, then immediately wished the word retracted, vanished, gone. *The trick I can never get right,* he said to himself; *This is the trick I can never seem to learn.*

ten

Peck spun briefly off center. Maybe it was the approach of fifty, perhaps the chirp of younger stars who, though not like Peck, nevertheless got compared to him. Perhaps it was people speaking of Peck reverently as "one of a kind" or a "classic" and making him feel like a painting in the Louvre or a novel published posthumously. Perhaps it was simply loneliness, possibly boredom, even impatience at feeling too similar for too long. He found himself looking back, remembering, longing. He thought about the kittens of the cats he'd employed in Hoboken.

Both Leigh and Lee were accepted at Yale. Leigh went, Lee decided to hold off. Grandfather Gow had grown blind due to a sudden assertion of dormant diabetes, so Lee went to live in the apartment Peck still kept above Low's to help his grandmother, now seventy-seven, cook. Lee said New York was filled with music. Why couldn't the city be his education? Peck felt both irritated and proud: proud to have a son in ways like himself, arrogant and naïve, but still irritated at Lee's arrogance and naïveté.

On the other hand, the decks were cleared. Space had

opened up. Peck's career had its periodic demands, but the channel was deep and obviously carved. He joked to J.T., "What does a classic do but hang in there, right?" J.T. had cut back. He'd moved to New Mexico to an expanse of mesa acreage somewhere between Taos and Los Alamos, where he'd begun making furniture. Punch had opened Trinity's, a restaurant. J.T. seemed peaceful, if that word could ever be applied to him. He said, "I haven't put my fist through a wall in years."

So, Peck had what some called latitude in his options, together with certain unchanneled energies. He played Vegas more. It made him feel vaguely rootless, which he both liked and hated. Some days he'd gamble. He could win or lose and it would be the same. Women approached. He felt complimented and he felt stupid. Some were his age, some younger, some beyond. He might be out by the pool at the Riviera and a conversation would start up. There'd be the dropping of some shoulder strap, an innuendo, an unambiguous proposition. At first the theater of it all was enough. Peck felt recharged, almost adequate, even desirable.

One is always teased, though, toward something—moments. And so there were times when Peck would find himself in an elevator heading up or down, to or from some consummation, almost always unhappy, disappointed, yet itchy: still itchy for an imagined level which never came. When he'd call Lee or Leigh from Las Vegas, they would hear his voice and always ask if he were out of the country. *You sound like you might be in Australia,* they'd say.

Once when he was playing the MGM Grand and before the evening's last show, a note appeared in Peck's dressing room which read: "Might an old friend say hello afterwards? I'll linger in the showroom." Who? Peck wondered. Who? And though he disliked second-guessing, shaping judgments, he made one nevertheless in the handwriting, in its figured printing, which seemed to be a woman's.

He performed better than usual, fueled by the adrenal of mystery. At one point, he made *himself* disappear, and the props which he'd been using for his effect floated and moved themselves in space, independently, completing the announced trick. It left the audience gasping at an illusion Peck had never before attempted. He wasn't quite sure how he'd done it. He reappeared in time to take the bow for a trick which had completed itself.

After the curtain, he waited, listening to the audience mill and wander out, watching stage hands box and store his paraphernalia. When the showroom seemed still, he stepped through the curtain to see whether the announced old friend was still there. She was. In an aisle toward the front stood a wheelchair. In the wheelchair was a woman, nicely gowned, hair rinsed a pastel blue, who sat poised.

"Hello, Peck," the woman said.

"Jesus, God," Peck said.

"You were wonderful," the woman said. "But I've said that before, haven't I? Often and gratefully in our history." She smiled.

Though he might not have recognized her had they walked past each other, her voice was unmistakable as something from a far earlier point in time. It was Leslie Fay. "I don't believe this," Peck said.

"What you never expect happens," Leslie Fay said. "I read that somewhere."

"Then it must be true," Peck said. "I never lie, but sometimes the truth disappears."

Leslie Fay laughed. Her laugh, too, had remained young.

She was sixty-three. An unkind version of sciatica had

made almost any walking impossible. Her husband, Michael, had ten years remaining on a prison sentence for illegal trafficking. After his conviction, she had lived briefly with a renaissance art historian who taught at Brandeis, a man for whom, she said, she felt deep, deep affection, but who was killed in a small Cessna plane crash. Would Peck escort her to her room on the seventeenth floor? She had a bottle of Remy Martin. Might they take a bath together for old time's sake?

They did, and Peck found it indescribably wonderful. He wept involuntarily for all the invisible conspiracy of memory and senses. Leslie's skin was still fine. Her body in the bath smelled like the body of the twenty-nine-year-old he had once bathed with. They kissed and touched each other. "I won't ask you to make love," Leslie Fay said. "Seeing you again has been more perfect than I could have schemed. I won't tamper with it." Peck understood. He lifted Leslie Fay from the bath, toweled and bore her gently to the bed, and kissed her good night.

"Good night, Peck," Leslie Fay said. And then she said something Peck found uncertain and curious. She said, "Things last."

Peck left.

A man named Gerald Fishbein contacted Peck about writing an "as-told-to" biography.

"Why?" Peck asked.

"Because you're amazing," Fishbein said. "Because you're a huge figure for so many people."

"I'm not literate enough to do it myself?" Peck queried.

"No, of course not. Of course you can, absolutely," Fishbein said. "It's just that in the world of words, I've been around. I know some of the ins and outs."

"Call me in five years," Peck said.

"Five years? What day?" Fishbein asked. He was trying to be funny.

"Tuesday," Peck said.

"Tuesday?" Fishbein said.

"Tuesday," Peck said.

"You got it!" Fishbein the biographer said and hung up.

Peck and Jessica kept on. She'd fly east, he'd fly west. The level of frustration never changed. They were like the little magnets kids played with, snapping together and flying apart. "We're doomed," Jessica said one night and then laughed. She'd been made a circuit judge. "I get to say these things now," she said, "because I'm a judge. I get to say things like *we're doomed* before I serve the sentence." She laughed. Peck groaned.

Peck went shopping and sent gifts to friends. That seemed a partial antidote. He started once-a-week facials and had his hair done every third day. He began exploring personal tailors. He learned wines, bought cases for what he told himself was a collection, began drinking the collection, all of course as an *ami de vin*. One night, his mother came to him in his sleep. She sat at her end of the table with a dry and empty glass and watched Peck finish off medoc after chardonnay. She looked abandoned and betrayed. The next morning Peck shipped almost all of his collection to Punch Dennis in New Mexico. "For Trinity's," his card said, "and its underground tests. Give the closest thing you've got to a bear hug to your scruffy husband."

So, Peck was ripe for what someone overdramatizing might call "a fall." And it came—*she* came—walking straight past him, down a beach in Mazatlan, her name Fiona Garrett. She was twenty years old and had thighs capable of an unreleasable hammerlock, skin that left the taste of totally leavened bread in Peck's mouth.

For the first time, Peck worried about a sex-induced heart attack. Fiona was tough and canny; she'd been an Air Force brat, girl of the month in at least two male magazines. She abused various controlled substances. For some reason, she liked Peck's company. The word "party" struck her reflex apparatus the way the scent of a fox hits certain dogs. Punch Dennis met her and called her "Peck's bimbo." It wasn't inappropriate and it spread.

Peck felt giddy, though. He liked the uncertainty and the sense of free-fall. Once again, though, part of his brain knew the induction to be artificial, and he felt age eleven: bold and magical, newly possible, even dangerous. Fiona got jewelry. She got clothes. She got a car. She kept saying *Marry me!* at theatrical peaks of her orgasms. Peck was sorely tempted. They drank shooters for two hours at the Frontier in Las Vegas, then staggered into a cab to "tie the knot." But Peck passed out beyond reviving. Nevertheless, when he came to, Fiona was giving him head and there was a marriage certificate tacked to their hotel wall. "That is not my handwriting," Peck said; "I did not sign that."

Fiona lasted five months and cost Peck over seventy thousand dollars, even more in personal damage and scarred personal connections. "I'm the last person who should call a friend a jerk," J.T. said, "but you've been a jerk."

Peck agreed.

For Lee it had been like a sudden wall of water pouring down a calm arroyo, the flood of tabloid candids and articles. Grandmother Gow would look limp and broken after unwrapping sea bass from a newspaper image of Peck and the corrupt Fiona. Lee would have to hold her. He resented his father's flagrant exposure and failure to imagine the hearts of others at risk, and Lee would rock his grandmother, sing to and comfort her. "It's just stupid," he would say; "it's just a stupid thing for stupid people who don't know any better."

Leigh was in her painting studio at Yale, working a color exercise, when a friend tossed the latest tabloid trash into the room. Yes, it was Peck's life, but it was theirs too, and how does one explain such a father to anyone—such a classic legend?

Peck finally came to his senses. What brought him there, sadly, was the death of Nick's Willie in a motorcycle accident. Nick reached Peck at a pool party in Santa Monica where things had gotten so out of control the band was trying to play underwater. "Oh shit, Nick, *no!*" Peck said. "Oh, Jesus!" He promised to catch the next plane. When he hung up, it occurred to him, standing there in the cruel and dingy froth of late-afternoon noise, that he had failed to tell his brother that he was sorry.

Willie's funeral was sad, indeed. He had gone his own way rebuilding cars, working in hotels and restaurants, living on the road, often with other motorcyclists. Dr. Peck, at eighty-five, wandered through the mourners, looking vacant and dazed. He kept asking: "It was Willie who died?"

Lanie was there with her new husband. Her eyes gaped like someone had bored holes into her head with a core-drill. "Excuse the medication," she said to Peck. Then she spoke of Patty, Nick's new wife. "Well, she does seem *sweet,*" she said. Both of Peck's twins came. Leigh stayed on his arm like a wife and was loving toward everyone. Lee was edgy and took swipes. "Where's the bimbo?" he asked. Then he apologized.

Peck waved away the question and, with it, Fiona. "People get confused," he said. "It happens to people."

Nicholas spoke. He said he felt he needed to, and it was an image Peck would never shake seeing his own little brother— their father's pride, mother's second-born, a husband before Peck married, a father before Peck and Victoria had children— who Peck had daily coaxed back onto his feet after his injury, now a three-hundred-pound man in a suit that was ill-fitting speaking through tears. The image held far too much and went in too many directions in and out of the void.

Willie had been a special child, Nicholas said. Always, from the first, there had been both more and less of him. Sometimes, Nick speculated, the more and the less got confused. He sometimes thought Willie's gifts were deficits and his deficits gifts. "Willie thought he had disappointed us when he made us proud. He would imagine he had swelled our hearts ... when he made them drop. ... And so, how do I say to my son now, this does not sort things out."

Back in Bedford three nights later, Peck felt a kind of gratitude that he could not begin to explain in detail. It broke onto him in a kind of pain and wonder, full-swollen with the privilege and responsibility of being a part of it. He cried for the people who had appeared and disappeared, who had meant so much to him. On the skin of his hands, he felt the weight and light of his mother's heart. The air around him seemed filled with ghosts, with sheen and music. He wondered if he might not be having some sort of *incident* ... a seizure, perhaps. He called Lee at Low's and asked whether he might come into the city to see him. Lee said yes.

Peck arrived the next day, mid-morning, and for nearly three hours, father and son prepared vegetables, saying little more than *Curl your fingers* or *How can you chop that fast?* Peck scrubbed pots. He rinsed rice. Mrs. Gow dealt with him in a sweet way; any rancor seemed as immaterial, in the face of his grating gingerroot, as steam.

After closing, Peck walked with his son to the cafe where he and Victoria had gone on their first date. He described the night. He described his feelings. He described his love. He held his teeth together to hold back some emotion, but couldn't. Lee worked his own lips like wet clay, pinching and twisting gargoyles with distorted spouts. The energy was nervous, but the emotions were hard to read. The scene Peck had envisioned would climax with the two of them holding each other in desperate love, spilling two snifters of Remy Martin in the process, but not caring. The climactic scene Peck got was ballooned with silence. It had Lee drumming his upper lip with his fingertips, stopping, sitting way back in his chair, lifting his cognac, smelling it, drinking it, wiping his lips with the back of his hand and nodding.

Where were they? What communication was there? Were they a better, a more promising father and son, than Peck and Dr. Peck? He couldn't tell.

Lee folded his hands together, fingers webbed in fingers. He leaned forward. He leaned back. He asked Peck if he would loan him two hundred thousand dollars. He wanted to open what he called a nouveau Chinese cuisine jazz club off Sheridan Square. He said it would be like a Mandarin Blue Note with four-star food and the best classical jazz musicians. "I've got a letter of intent from Herbie Mann," he told his father. Peck said he would set up an account at Chemical Bank.

Peck began to relearn his essential solitude. J.T. turned down a fifth *DETAILS AT TEN* picture. He said he was happier working a wood lathe; he didn't know if he would ever act again. Peck's twins were busy. Leigh finished Yale and went immediately to New Mexico to live and paint in a caretaker's cottage on J.T.'s property. Lee opened what got called Lee Low's. Peck didn't receive an invitation—Lee said it was an oversight. Peck went anyway and was impressed by the unbelievably good Peking duck, shrimp wrapped in nappa cabbage, and a haunting jazz violin trio.

Peck read scripts for possible movies. At fifty-four, he had to read with a certain humility and re-evaluation. The roles were either residual roles from fifteen years before or for indomitable geriatrics. Some nights he cried for Victoria and what they might still be sharing at this point. Some nights he longed for Fiona or even a Fiona look-alike. He and Jessica talked for hours long distance. They'd talk like sister and brother, mother and child. Often she would be at some function, some board meeting, some fund raising event, and he would ramble without cause to her machine.

Though his better judgment advised against it, he let a network producer flatter him into trying *Radio Magic* as a television special. The network spared no expense. They lined up a who's who of guest stars. They promoted powerfully, having Peck on the *Tonight* show twice, his hair coiffed into a thick silvering mane, and acting sly and artful as he produced "the Atlantic Ocean" from the famous host's pant leg: a scrolled poster which, unrolled, ended up being a photo of the pier at Santa Monica. "Whoops, the Pacific!" Peck quipped: "I can never get this trick right."

Still, the whole charm of *Radio Magic* was that it lay beyond any audience vision, and though the media critics were kind, even though they indulged Peck with their "pure original" and "still unrivaled" appellations, Peck himself felt old and half-assed, cheap and foolish. He was told the show was fourth in the overall ratings for the week. He should have been happy with that, but he hated hearing it. He hated that some good part of his imagination had been sacrificed for what he felt was a pathetic replica.

Dr. Peck called Peck in Bedford. At the age of eighty-seven, he was giving up medicine. That morning, he had forgotten the name of a patient who had been seeing him for twenty-two years. *Connell Carver!* it came finally. But there was no longer any excuse. Think of it. No, impossible, that was it. Connell Carver was, after all, an emeritus professor of English literature at Harvard.

"So, what will you do?" Peck asked.

"I don't know. I thought possibly I'd make jokes or do magic," his father said.

"Good shot. Touché!" Peck said. "Work on the timing, though. You could improve the timing, as always. Still, it's a good start."

"Nicholas says I can run the developer at his clinic."

Peck tried to imagine the older Dr. Peck working for his son. "Tell Nick I said good luck," Peck laughed.

Two weeks later, Nick called to say their father had overdosed on anti-depressants. "I came by to take him out for fettucini with clam sauce and found him on his bed with half a pulse," Nick said. "He's in the General. He'll be okay. He seems mad at himself for botching the thing. There's a lot of toxicity still in his system. It's hard to know how rational or irrational he's being."

"I'll get the shuttle," Peck said. "I'll be right up."

He flew in. "He's terrorizing the ward," Nick said. "There's nothing worse than a doctor in his own hospital. Talk about wanting to be God and wanting it both ways. He's got the perfect setup: patient and doctor."

Peck tiptoed into his father's room. If he were resting, he didn't want to rouse him.

"Which one are you?" his father said. His face looked pink and altered and angry—uncentered and sagging without its wirerim glasses.

"Take your pick," Peck said.

His father ranted about how every doctor should serve time, "and I don't mean on rounds," he said. "We're all frauds! We think we're the panther's meow, but we're all hoaxes."

"I've been saying that for years," Peck said.

"Shut up!" his father said.

Their talk hiked an unpredictable path. There was the expected parrying. At times, though, his father was extraordinarily vulnerable and open. "I act modest," he told Peck, "but it's hard for me to be challenged."

"You can be tough," Peck said, matching the candor, "but God knows I can be willful, too."

"God knows," his father said, then added as an afterthought that he was bored. "Entertain me," he said. "Show me a trick."

Peck produced a nurse.

"Wrong color," his father said.

"You're a bigot," Peck scolded his father.

"Do a real trick. Make the ghost dance!"

Peck stayed in town for nearly a week "to see how he's weathering things," he told Nick. His father was up and down, pungent and confused. "I don't think Harvard's the same place as when I went there," he would begin and launch into a half-hour diatribe of nostalgia, insight, rearrangement of names and history. It was hard for Peck to get a read on the precise course of his father's recovery.

He stayed with Nicholas and Patty in Lexington during his

visit. Nick wanted that. Patty was sweet, always, and indulgent. She worshiped Nick and seemed perhaps too grateful for the life of a doctor's wife. "She's not Lanie!" Nick would say, cued by nearly anything, "Still—"

Peck had to agree. Patty would occasionally speak ungrammatically (*Nick don't mind when I do this*) and a twitch would electrify Peck's back. He found himself aware he had certain prejudices, that he was—surprise!—his father's child. One night when she had gone to bed and Peck and Nick sat watching a second Celtics overtime, Peck spoke to the snacking Nick about his weight.

"I've tried," Nick said. "I think Patty likes me fat. Do you ever hear from your bimbo?"

Peck was not psychic. He had never seriously attempted that. Still, he imagined himself speaking at Nick's funeral.

One day, on an impulse it was hard to find the origin of, Peck asked his father if, once he was released from the hospital, he might like to come and live with Peck in Bedford. "I'm all alone there," he mused. "It's a big house. You could move your own furniture down if it would make you feel more at home."

"You don't know what you're inviting," his father said.

"Well, I went through the ward and asked all the other patients if they'd be my roommate," Peck said, "and no takers. You know these parties where you send out fifty invitations and three people come?"

On the last day of Peck's visit, Dr. Peck said yes, although he said he had reservations. He thought they could try it out if he could have a couple of weeks to make arrangements. He'd let Peck know.

There was a message on Peck's machine when he got back. It was Jessica sounding unusually coy. He called, and she was flirtatious and evasive. "What I was hoping was to get right to the point with this ... ah ... verdict," she said, "but that's not the way it's coming out." Her agenda was that she'd decided to take a year's leave of absence from the bench. "It just seemed like the time," she said. What she proposed was to fly back and move in with Peck. "I think it's time for us," she said.

Peck was speechless.

"Hello? ..." Jessica tried.

"Sure," Peck said. "I mean, sure." He drew a blank about his father.

"It seems we've put this off and played with it for quite a while, don't you think?" Jessica said.

"I do," Peck agreed. "I do, certainly. Quite a while— played."

"Do I need to bring anything?" she asked. "My pajamas? A sleeping bag? Muffin tins?"

"I have everything but a cordless screwdriver," Peck said.

"In that case," she said she'd call Peck with flight information.

Within the week, Dr. Peck called to say Nick could drive him down the following Thursday and that a moving van would follow. "Great!" Peck said.

That was on Monday. On Tuesday, Leigh called to say she was having her *first show of paintings ever—a two-person show* at a gallery in Santa Fe in six weeks. Would Peck fly in for the opening?

"I wouldn't miss it," he said.

She was thrilled. "Lee's wrong about you," she said.

Peck said he appreciated her confidence: "What is he wrong about?" he asked.

"Oh, you know Lee," she said.

"Possibly not," Peck returned.

"He gets confused." Leigh laughed, and they hung up.

The next morning, Jessica called to give him her flight times. She would be arriving on Saturday. "I'm a little bit nervous," she confessed.

"Piece of cake," Peck said. He started to sweat. He mentioned nothing about his father. Once he'd hung up, he roamed his house, going from room to room, listening to the choking and shuddering of his furnace, observing the way light fell through his windows. Was there a name for this—this time in a person's life when a son fathered his father and the son began living with his high school sweetheart? Where would he put whom? Was a fourteen-room house large enough? Perhaps he could just leave the details to Mrs. Nielsen.

Eleven

nick's Volvo pulled up the drive on the appointed Thursday almost on the hour. "You've got guests!" Mrs. Nielsen called to Peck, who was at the window.

Guests, Peck thought. He watched his brother and father roll out of the car.

"He's been a prick," Nick said, out of the side of his mouth to Peck, "the whole way."

"We've been having a spelling bee!" Dr. Peck announced. "Nicholas either won't or can't spell *obese.*"

"O-B-E-S-E. Obese," Nick spat.

"Hey, Pop. Welcome! Welcome to your new home," Peck said and tried to encircle his father.

"Where's the van?" Dr. Peck said, craning his neck left and right, pushing Peck away. "The van's not here yet?"

"Good luck," Nick said and spread a hand on Peck's back. Then to their father, he said: "Pop, I'm sorry, but I have to turn and head back. I said I'd be there this afternoon. You know doctors."

"How much is the fare?" Dr. Peck asked Nicholas.

Nick and Peck looked at each other. "The fare?" Nick asked.

"Ask the driver how much the fare is," Dr. Peck said to Peck, and then: "Where's the van? They said they'd be here by the time I arrived."

Nick left. Peck hauled his father's suitcases to the allotted area of the house—three rooms in a re-arranged apartment combination—he and Mrs. Nielsen had set up, and told his father he had paid the fare. "What do I owe you?" Dr. Peck wanted to know. "What's the monthly rent, I've forgotten. I need my desk. Will I have an icebox? Where's the van?"

"What say we have some lunch," Peck suggested.

"Just maybe a cup of borscht," his father chimed. "I'm not really that hungry."

When the van arrived two hours later, Dr. Peck was in an advanced state of agitation. He also seemed to have lost track of the fact that Peck was his son. Every other sentence concerned costs and finances. "I need to call my attorney," he kept saying. "I need to set up a checking account and have money transferred. I'll give you a shopping list. How many residents live here?

Once the furniture was in place, arranged very much as it had been in the family house in Dr. Peck's corner with his desk, chair, coffee table, and books on the shelf precisely as they'd been next to the chair, along with his lamp, his bed, his prize oriental rugs, the confusion seemed to clear up. Peck was obviously his son. Nicholas had driven him down. Weren't the van people good to bring things in as quickly as they had? What was for supper? He was starved. Could Dr. Peck take Peck out, maybe to a good Hunan restaurant if there was one. Peck liked Chinese, didn't he? Dr. Peck couldn't describe Peck's kindness in welcoming an aging parent and making him feel so much at home.

That evening in front of the fireplace, sharing Tanqueray and tonics, Peck conjured the thought that this could be grand.

There's no reason it can't be an opportunity, a second chance to master one of life's most difficult tricks: a son's relationship with his father, he thought.

The following morning after breakfast, Dr. Peck blurted into some anxious talk about his lawyer and money. "Have we known each other a while?" he asked his son. "When did we meet?"

That afternoon, Gerald Fishbein, the biographer, called Peck. "It's Tuesday," he said. "Five years."

"The real moments in my life are still to come," Peck advanced. "So if you'll give me another five years."

"No prob."

"And make it a Thursday next time, okay?"

"Five years, Thursday. You got it!" Fishbein said.

Jessica arrived as announced by plane on Saturday. Peck watched and felt jolted as she exited the jetway. Age had settled in with her in a way that gave her a classic beauty. It made Peck's breath jump. Driving back to Bedford from LaGuardia, Peck ventured the details about his father. "Well, this should be ... what? What should it be? What's the word?"

"Interesting?"

"Interesting will do."

"Not dull," Jessica agreed. "Are your plans for us to share a room—you and me, that is; I don't mean me and your father—or will I be a mysterious woman down the hall?"

"I thought I'd broach that with you as an option," Peck said.

"An option to live down the hall?" Jessica asked. She smiled and added, "When did you start using words like *broach* anyway?"

Dr. Peck loved the cello, and so before dinner, they all

drank Glenlivet and shared chopped liver on triscuits, Boccherini playing in the background. Peck re-introduced everyone. "Oh, yes, the dentist's daughter," Dr. Peck said. "Is business brisk?" Without a lost beat, Jessica announced that her father had been dead for six years. "It's the damn nitrous oxide," Dr. Peck said. "It's unstable, you know. He's not the first." Then Dr. Peck asked whether the two of them were going to a dance that evening. Wasn't that what they usually did—go to a dance and then neck a little afterwards?

Peck said he thought they'd probably stay in.

He and Jessica tried out Peck's room and bed. Peck opened the three drawers he'd cleared in the birdseye maple dresser. "So, you're taking the top and I'm on the bottom?" Jessica quipped.

Peck didn't have an answer. "I have one request," Jessica said, shaking out her hair. From an inside pocket of one of her suitcases, she produced two scented candles. "Light these while I get ready," she said. Then she disappeared, nightclothes in hand, into the master bathroom.

Peck lit the candles. One was red, one gold, and as their flames snaked and leapt, they laced the room with spice. Memory and closeted feelings broke loose and seemed to scamper like small creatures into dark corners, climb the walls, beat like quiet moths on the ceiling. Peck looked at his bed. Spread on it was a quilt Victoria had pieced over time; it had been a project of several years.

The bathroom door opened and Jessica moved out. "I brought just my flannel nightgown and this lace thing," she said, holding the lace thing out in her hand. "Confronted by the moment and the mirror, it really wasn't a hard decision."

Peck told her she looked beautiful. "That's your line," she said, "you remembered it. Good." Peck said he meant it. She thanked him, then moved to and against him for a kiss. But there was too much in the room: too much time, too much feeling, and Peck felt his head getting dizzy. *Where was he? Who was he kissing?*

He pulled the covers aside so they could slide in. Jessica moved in to him. Peck's breath caught. His head felt wide and echoing, it felt haunted like an old New England house. He noticed the wallpaper Victoria had chosen and hung, the ceiling she had painted herself with ivory semigloss. Peck put his hands on Jessica's shoulders and found it remarkable how open the whole of her body seemed, even the bones of the shoulders, which he set resistance against.

"Problem?" she asked. He said there seemed to be. "Well, that's us," she said. "One of us is ready, the other isn't. It's old stuff. Why should we expect it to be different?"

Peck could see her smile in the candlelight. It was hard to tell whether the smile was sweet or angry. "It's just, … this was Victoria's and my bed," Peck said.

"Peck," Jessica said. She rotated her back to him, bumping him perhaps too hard in his midsection with her rump. "You don't need to voice it."

It was about three or four hours later, in what Peck's mother used to call "the wee hours," when Peck heard a terrible scream from the driveway. He leapt up, rushed to his window. Jessica was bolt upright and confused. "What? …"

Outside, lit essentially by himself, was Antony Foley on fire. Peck grabbed a quilt from the bed, raced down the stairs, jumped onto the blazing human, knocking him down, and rolled the fire out.

At the local emergency ward an hour later, Antony explained that his intention had been *refenge* with a molotov cocktail. He had lit the fuse, dipped it into a Gallo wine bottle, cocked his arm, and then all the kerosene and the fire with it had flowed out onto him. He thanked Peck for saving his life. "I've seen the light," he told Peck.

Peck told him it was a bad joke. Jessica, who had come along, elbowed him. Antony said he hadn't meant it as a joke. He was going to change his life—*really* change his life this time—and be good. He asked Peck if he would come and see him again before he left the hospital. Peck said he would.

Driving back to the farm, Jessica had to know something. "Is this pretty much the way you live?" she asked.

The next morning at breakfast, Dr. Peck confessed to being confused. "Didn't you used to be Chinese?" he asked Jessica.

It was sweet and frustrating—the next weeks, the next span of time. Peck and Jessica certainly loved one another. They shared the same bed, they fell into each other's routines and habits and considerations in a remarkable fit. Yet of a given night, Jessica's hands would be on Peck, and Peck would stay them—hold and quiet them. The next night his would be on her, and she might leave the bed, stand by the window, stare out, tell Peck she didn't understand it entirely, that she was sorry.

Dr. Peck grew progressively more disoriented. Peck was alternately the physician's son, the landlord, and the "movie star who had a room there." His father related to him variously in all three roles. Mrs. Nielsen remained stalwart and patient. She buffed the zone between Peck, the caretaking son, and Peck, the groping and uncertain suitor. She guided the elder Peck back to bed when he arose after only two hours' sleep looking for breakfast. Peck gave her bonuses. He gave bonuses on top of bonuses. "Oh, Mr. Peck," she would say and thank him.

The time came for Leigh's opening in Santa Fe. Mrs. Nielsen said she and the doctor would be fine, that they had become good friends. Peck and Jessica flew west.

J.T. had assured Peck that he and Punch would meet them curbside, outside the baggage claim at the Albuquerque airport, and there they were, but on horseback, with two extra saddled horses beside them.

"Climb aboard!" J.T. barked. He indicated a waiting sky cab: "Give your bags to this gentleman, he has instructions."

Jessica rose to the moment's theater and its challenge. She swung herself up. Peck did likewise. "Follow us!" J.T. said.

In fact, they had a horse trailer in the express parking lot. Jessica feigned disappointment. "I thought we were going to ride into the desert and do peyote," she said.

Peck nudged her. "Don't give him ideas."

"Hey, I'm a pillar!" J.T. said. "I don't do stuff like that any more. Now your *daughter,* on the other hand!"

"I don't want to know," Peck said.

"Just kidding. She's great," Punch said, putting her own cap on the banter. "Fabulous. Lovely. Powerful. And her show is impressive."

The reunion was sweet. Leigh was in her makeshift studio finishing one final canvas. She threw a cloth over it. "You can't see it," she told Peck. "You can't see any of them, you have to wait two days."

Leigh knew Jessica. Time had made them friends, they were easy. They hugged.

Jessica announced that Leigh should put *herself* on exhibition. What could be more beautiful? Peck and Jessica met Punch and J.T.'s two mixed-blood foster children, Nina and Lane, and were then escorted to a separate guest house.

At sunset, the five adults hiked the abutting mesa carrying Tecate beer in their hands. The coyotes had already started and the sun went fuchsia. They returned and drove out to the Rancho de Chimayo for dinner. Punch said it was the friskiest she'd seen her husband in months. The two old friends got drunk on margaritas, which led to improvised songs backed by the house band. They ended with one, which they announced to all, was for a third friend named Russell who couldn't join them that evening; it was a song, they announced, that Russell had written. And then, together, Peck and J.T. made up a song that sounded like one Russell might have composed, singing it full out and ending in tears.

Jessica snuggled against Peck in the car and told him it had been a most wonderful evening. Peck had touched her with his curious spirit and open affections. An hour later, in the clay-colored and moonish dark of the guest house, the two joined for the first time—two people who had thought of such a moment, who had considered and imagined it for forty years. Peck said *finally,* Jessica *at long last,* almost simultaneously. It was the sweetest, most unhurried, most unselfconscious lovemaking that Peck had ever known.

Somewhere near three a.m., J.T. knocked on their door. Nick had called. Dr. Peck had attacked Mrs. Nielsen with a graphite tennis racquet. She was all right, but he'd gone pretty crazy. "Oh shit!" Peck said and asked what the present situation was.

"Nick said he had some local constable staying round-the-clock until you get there. He said you need to get home tomorrow."

"Look, I'm not missing my daughter's show," Peck said. He called Nicholas. "Go over there and cover for me. It's your turn," he said.

Nick pleaded a crunch, a serious backlog at the clinic.

Peck said this was Nick's problem for the next four days,

that he was sorry but his own priorities for the next four days were the images Leigh had made with her heart and hands. He told Nick to find whoever he had to cover for him, get in his too-expensive car, and drive his "fat ass" down to Bedford.

Nick got angry. "Some of us have work more than just gigs," he said.

Peck got angry. "Well, maybe the constable will go home and Pop will wander off into the foothills like an old elephant and die there."

"You know something, you're a prick," Nick said.

"I get Pop full-time. All I'm asking is for you to bail me out this once."

The two calmed down. Nick said he could have Dr. Peck hospitalized for up to a week, that he had power of attorney.

"Do it, then. It's a great solution," Peck said. "He'll thrive in a hospital."

As it had been at Willie's funeral and after Jessica had come to live with Peck, the next days held clusters and constellations of life that flashed and surged like massive electrical fronts of weather. Peck realized he was a son and a father, a lover, best friend, child, and adult. It was stunning and breathtaking, even mysterious. It moved him, made him speechless. Many of Leigh's paintings were of her mother. It made Peck so proud, it broke his heart. Jessica told him, looking at the intricate and tender portrayals of Victoria, that she felt she should leave. Peck pulled her tight: "No," he said, "please, no."

The night following Leigh's show, Peck and Jessica made love with even more sweetness and fervor. "Something's *in* you," Jessica said.

"I've never had a set-up like that," Peck parried. "It's too easy." They laughed.

Peck cried at the airport thinking of the power of his daughter and the power of his friend, for the landscapes he'd been living in and the power of caring, which seemed newly cemented between Jessica and himself. They flew home. *Why do I call it home?* Peck wondered.

At the hospital, Dr. Peck raged at his son for the inadequate facilities and nursing care; he said the charts were badly kept and he would see that certain people were dismissed. Peck called Nicholas. They agreed it was time for a full-care home and congratulated themselves on having been brave enough to even try the experiment. "I'm sorry we said the things we did to each other. I regret them."

"I regret them too," Peck said.

And so, Dr. Peck went to Leander Manor near Bedford. As Jessica contemplated the end of her "leave of absence," she began talking about marriage. They discussed it and decided their unsettled status with one another was somehow part of the love, the ongoing passion. It was, after all, their history. They pledged as much time together as circumstances would allow.

At La Guardia, in the September of their parting, Peck confessed that "airports are getting to be brutal."

"Soon," Jessica said, and then, "thank you."

Work seemed an answer to the melancholy Peck felt in a suddenly empty house. His films, comedy, magic, and special appearances answered a need to feel anchored. He did a "best of" album and tape. HBO asked for an hour, which had the modest ambition of being, in its producer's words, the classic Peck hour. In one part, a haunting ten-minute segment, what Peck conjured at his fingertips through the spirits of technology were images (some still, some moving) of his mother, father, brother, wife, children, as well as of the Gows, who had died within two months of one another, and of some of his closest friends. Literally out of the void, like strange and touching holograms, those dearest to Peck came alive like spring flowers in the enchanted air.

Perhaps most touching and unnerving among the phantoms living there in the palm of Peck's hand was Dr. Peck in footage from Leander Manor, alternately nostalgic and then mistaking Peck for an orderly. Reviews talked about the *new* Peck. Some applauded, some said he had moved his concept of comedy and magic beyond good taste.

Peck did some laconic interviews. He did two films. He stayed for month-long periods with Jessica, watched her in her judicial robes at court, and found himself falling in love again. She was splendid at everything she did. She came back to visit in Bedford. They traveled to Russia together, bought a cooperative on Key Biscayne.

Lee opened a new restaurant, Lee Low's West, which Peck helped finance. Peck wondered off and on about Lee's sexuality. Could a life be just food and music? It struck Peck that Lee never mentioned friends or partners. He seemed, nevertheless, to be at peace with himself, and Low's West featured paintings by Leigh, which pleased Peck. He hoped it said something about a mutual sense of caring among the twins. Leigh had shows in Los Angeles and San Francisco, Dallas, and Denver. She secured a gallery in New York, bought a house north of Taos. Meanwhile, Peck turned sixty.

During February of Peck's sixty-first year, he got called to the phone from his trailer on the set of a comic movie he was making about Noah's ark. It was Patty with news that Nicholas had been struck down shoveling show—a valvular lesion. Peck started to wail *No, God no!* He had *warned* Nicholas! *Jesus!* What was wrong with these damned doctors? They lived beyond their brilliance and shunned the basic principals of good health. Better to be a cook like Lee, better to paint pictures. Better to be a magician. Peck apologized to Patty for his outburst. It was, he said, because he loved Nicholas more than he knew, more than he realized. He would fly up immediately.

"You called him *Nicholas,*" Patty said.

"I know, that's his name."

"But you almost always called him *Nick.*"

"Well—"

"Where did *Nicholas* come from?"

Out of the void, Peck thought. He knew he was in a period of his life, with their father in tow from Leander Manor, when he could see elements of certain situations one might judge as comic. *Who died?* Dr. Peck, eighty-six in his Brooks Brothers suit that hung like sackcloth, kept asking. *Was it Peck?*

"No, *I'm* Peck," Peck reiterated. "It was *Nicholas.*"

Their father kept wanting it to be Peck. *Did you say Peck?* he boomed.

Jessica, who had flown in and was on Peck arm, asked, "Doesn't this hurt?"

"I don't think so," Peck said. "Possibly it does, I'm not sure. It makes me sad, though, certainly sad. I can say that much. Isn't that weird?"

At Mt. Auburn Cemetery, graveside, some instinct triggered Peck to look behind him, and there, on a rise slightly separated, were Lee and Leigh, clearly studying the two generations at graveside, their father and grandfather. Both of the twins looked uncertain and vaguely stunned. Peck knew the look. He had seen it in audiences over a lifetime. Their bafflement clearly went deeper, like some geologic probe. Peck wasn't even sure what they had seen, what illusion had so caught their consideration.

At Nicholas's home, at the post-burial gathering, Dr. Peck scanned the crowd. "So many former patients," he said.

"Do you feel old?" the twins asked their father, independent of one another. Peck considered. At first he said that he wasn't sure, but then said no. He said his emotions felt very crowded—whatever that meant—and overcharged, but that he didn't think he felt *old*.

Peck went back to Hannibal, Missouri, to the film he'd left, to play Noah and make people laugh. Ten minutes after they'd shot the dove's arrival with a minibottle ("It's a cheap joke," Peck warned), news came that Dr. Peck had been taken, finally, by a mild pneumonia. The illness was *the old person's friend,* Peck remembered his father having said. The words on the yellow telegram paper skated like waterbugs. They were sad, unexpected, shocking, and yet mundane and even welcome.

He thought that no one beats the Big Magician in the Sky for surprise. Even the probable appears out of synch and too sudden. Still, he thought the invisible magician could do a lot better with shape and balance. There was too much *into* the void and not enough *out* of it. Take away the calla lilies, okay. But if you do that, bring in the flaming deserts, the peacocks, the doves! Surprise is good, surprise is the essence. But for every sigh, there be a gasp, Peck thought.

Nevertheless, and stagecraft withstanding, it was curious how strange Peck felt at his father's funeral, as if he were in his forties again and nimble, pliant, and unburdened. How should that be? An unsettling wave of guilt broke over him and then washed away just as quickly.

Again, Peck returned to the Noah set—just in time to see the waters recede. He convinced the director to fly J.T. in so he could lead the animals from the ark: "He's fabulous," Peck said, "with creatures. Fabulous!" On the appointed morning, though, the animals vanished. "Funny," J.T. said, "very funny." Peck just grinned. "Where did they go?" the film's line producer asked. Peck shrugged. "What did you expect from a magician?" In the released film, nevertheless, one sees J.T. guiding the endless tethers of paired beasts: afghan hounds, hummingbirds, unicorns, stegosauri, his two foster children costumed as Halloween vampires.

As they had years before in Corfu, Peck and J.T. stayed on briefly in Hannibal because the opportunity was there. They took a riverboat trip. They drank Hennessy in the moonlight, remembering, putting pieces back that had once been, wondering about pieces that might have been rearranged. They were two men who were ultimately grateful for what their mortal years had delivered. "Finally, there's earth and water," J.T. said.

"And a few good punch lines," Peck said.

The two friends smiled. J.T. asked if Peck had ever been a chauvinist. "In my youth," Peck said, then rolled his eyes. "In my youth! What am I talking about?"

Two months later, on the same Tuesday, first Leigh then Lee called in Bedford to announce wedding plans.

"Whoa!" was all that Peck could manage with the second announcement.

"*Whoa?*"

"Or something like 'whoa.' So, this is serious?"

"Dad!" Leigh laughed.

"I mean, it's not … you mean, it's serious?"

"Of course it's serious. What else could it be?"

"It could be, I could be—I don't know. It could be serious, and it could be let's get Dad."

"It's serious."

"I'm surprised—okay? I don't know why, but surprised. Did you guys coordinate?" Peck asked, then admitted to having given up hoping.

"Hoping what?" Lee said.

"Hoping to be able to—who can say—whatever; never mind," Peck said. He thought he sounded impatient and cranky like his father.

"Hoping for *little* Pecks?" Leigh asked.

"Okay; okay, you've got the old man over a barrel," Peck said. "Enjoy it. Be my guest."

"Thank you," Leigh said, "I will. It's fun."

And Peck felt the uncanniness of lineage. "Well," he ventured, "there's a rule of nature, of course, that comes into play here."

"Really?" Leigh said. "What's that?"

"You get to surprise me more and more."

"I'll look forward to it," Leigh said.

After the call, Peck put on his down jacket and went for a walk. The apples in the orchard were two months past and the ground was full of them, and the October air smelled like ripe wood and cider. Peck moved briskly. He breathed the afternoon in, he breathed it out. He had known of Leigh's two-year romance with a poet named Christopher Merrit. Peck had had no glimmer, though, of Lee's involvement with a Chinese dress designer. "Again?" Peck had asked to fix her name. "Alicia Kong," Lee had said.

Peck was sixty-two years old, his wife deceased, both parents gone. He had a dear and living friend, another dear friend and lover with whom he didn't live, a brother passed on, and a best friend. Two active and successful (as much as he hated the word) children were both planning marriage. Peck laid claim to his basic jots there beneath the late October sky. He found his eyes awash with curious gratitude for being who he was and having had this life. "Sentiment!" he chided himself. "Sentiment, Jesus!" Still, he was glad for it.

+welve

he invitations were on rice paper. Jessica came in from California. J.T. and Punch flew in from New Mexico. Patty and Nicholas's children drove down from Massachusetts and New Hampshire with their families, including three towheaded mites who called Patty *Gramma*. Peck had the queer feeling of being an underachiever.

It was, of course, a double wedding, held at the farm. The brides and grooms all wore cutaways. Everyone's hair fell just shoulder length. "They may be making a point," Peck speculated, although he couldn't say what point that may have been.

"Don't make any of us disappear," Leigh said, moving close, kissing her father's cheek.

"You'll disappear soon enough," Peck said. "You know that. You don't need me."

The barn served as the chapel. It was December, and with the lowing of the animals, it seemed like a Christmas pageant. Peck felt his chest flutter and his eyes swarm, once with the offering of his daughter and once again with the vows. He thought how different ceremonies were from performances, how truer the spell and how much more enchanted. Jessica kept placing her hand on the flat of his back, which seemed stabilizing.

He felt happy with his children's chosen. He approved of them. He liked his daughter's new name, Leigh Merrit, and approved of her poet husband, who was so full of brightness and possibility, looking athletic, angelic, and just remarkably young. Alicia Kong, too, looked tempered and elegant, so precise in her beauty, so sure in carriage and speech.

The Kongs, in general, knew how to charm. Their daughter's comfort in living seemed their gift. Wellington Kong was an architect in Philadelphia, Priscilla an internist. Both gave themselves to laughter and openness in ways Peck immediately cherished and envied. Wellington called Peck "the master of the unexpected," and Peck felt he'd never had so pleasing a review. "I may steal it for my headstone," he quipped.

"Are we in a period of mortality jokes now?" Lee asked.

"It was a transition," Peck said, "just a transition, not a joke. There's a difference."

"What's he talking about, do you know?" Lee asked his sister.

The Merrits, conversely, were ill at ease. Charles was a banker in Alexandria, Virginia. His father had been a banker. Lucy Merrit repeated words like *board* and *guild* frequently. They gave the impression Christopher's life choice might have been defiant and a cruel disappointment. *Poetry* was a word that dropped like a spider down some malicious strand. That he was getting married in a barn to a half-Asian painter, whose father was a comedian, was too much for them to bear. The Merrits kept glancing at one another with a look that said *Can we endure this?*

Still, none of the Merrits' disease caught at the fabric of the celebration. The ceremony itself held a magic that Peck had never practiced, only known in intimacy. Lee played a composition on the harp; Leigh unveiled a painting, *Epithalamion*, done of the four, semi-nude, holding hands, in an enchanted circle.

Punch Dennis had insisted on catering as "a donation" from Trinity's, so all the food was Southwestern: a champagne mixed with margaritas that lifted the hair on everyone's neck, an amazing salsa, an addictive guacamole. There were carnitas and fajitas and chimichangas. The entire barn rose and drifted in a carbonation of champagne and cilantro. Music brewed from a mariachi band. Sadly, the elder Merrits, Charles and Lucy, slipped away fairly early on. Peck saw hurt in his new son-in-law's eyes and in the soft corners of his mouth as he watched his parents leave. A car revved somewhere in the crisp pastoral night beyond and Peck saw Christopher's registry of it—of the sound, the signal—that made him close his eyes briefly, then decide that the night was his, after all, as was his life ahead. His good spirit rushed in, his color, his smile.

A cry went up late, as the night and its joy were drifting on, for Peck and J.T. to perform. But they declined. "I'm just the aging father." Peck said.

"I'm the father's aging friend," J.T. chimed.

Jessica stayed on, as planned, after the weddings, through the holidays, and until the second day of the new year. "I'm treating myself," she said, "to the illusion that your family are my family, that your house is mine."

Abracadabra, Peck said.

It was perhaps the sweetest, most balanced time Peck and Jessica had ever shared. They chose a tree and strapped it to the roof of Peck's Subaru and drove it home. "I almost feel as though we should name it," Jessica said.

"Tree," Peck offered.

"Christmas," Jessica said.

"Better."

They strung Christmas with lights and decorations while sipping Kir Royales and listening to live Renaissance Festival music.

"We've never done this," Jessica said. Her voice sounded uncertain, skeptical.

"This?" Peck inquired, pursuing her pronoun.

"This kind of normal family thing."

"So?" Peck asked.

"So, why does it feel like we have," she wondered, "like we've been doing this for at least forty years?"

They sat together remembering, casting back to draw up moments, dismayed at what Peck called their former selves. They felt delighted and even touched—giddy and proud. They made love under a comforter Peck had bought years previously on a film trip he'd made to Ireland. They cuddled and made aimless, fully fatuous talk, the tree lights painting their clear skins like a dancehall globe. They watched the news on television: a bridge collapse near Baltimore, a cease-fire in the Middle East, a catalogue of basketball scores. They made love a second time.

"How old are we?" Jessica asked.

Peck laughed. "Too old for this, probably" he said.

"Are we supposed to even be able to do this? Do you think we've just shortened our lives? Or have we added to them?"

On New Year's Day, Peck got a call from Gerald Fishbein, the biographer. "I'm persistent," he said. Peck had to agree. "It's my virtue," Fishbein said in a halting self-promotion.

Peck invited him up the following week.

"He wants to what?" Jessica asked. "… to do *what*?" Jessica was leaving for California, and they were approaching the airport when Peck explained. She wondered why Peck couldn't write his own biography.

"I've tried," he said. "All the verbs vanished."

She groaned.

"All the nouns changed to adjectives."

"Yes, I've seen you do that," Jessica said, "and it is an illusion." She felt sweetly suckered. "And so, who is this Gerald Fishbein? Do you know anything at all about him?"

"He's a kind of shadow, I think," Peck said, "or has been for the last few years. He wants my life. He wants to boil my notorious life down into a few words and make a killing."

"Be careful," Jessica warned. An hour later, she said it again, *"Be careful,"* before she turned and faded into the telescope connecting the airport to her 767. It was a vanishing trick, seeing her fade from sight, and forceful enough to blindside Peck and cross him with a curious combination of chills. He stared at her absence, into the air where she'd been, hungrily staring. *Would he ever see her again?* he wondered. Of course he would, but the question had never come to him before, and there it was. He said her name, *Jessica.*

Fishbein drove a large flatbed truck that inched forward up Peck's Bedford drive with a host of racked clatters and wheezes. "Oncology on wheels!" he said, presenting his transportation. "Even the rust metastasizes!"

"Interesting metaphors," Peck observed.

"I call her ICU!" Fishbein announced. "It's a double play on words."

"Have you been to medical school?" Peck asked.

"Two months, University of Cincinnati."

"Thank you for explaining," Peck said. "How old are you?"

Fishbein, who was a man without guile, admitted he was twenty-seven. He had called Peck when he was a junior at Haverford because Peck had been his hero since he was eleven. He compared Peck to Columbus: "One minute there's no New World and the earth is flat, the next—it's right before your eyes!—*abracadabra!* and there's an America in sight and we're riding on a spinning ball. It's never the trick you start, it's the trick you end with, and it's better."

"Nicely said," Peck offered.

They drank hot cider and Fishbein promised he didn't wish to push anything. Honor was his motive, not profits. "There's time," he said. He told Peck of the two books he'd published since Haverford, which he'd *cut his teeth on.* Both were biographies. One was the life of a Latin American poet, the other of a sculptor who was famous for using a chain saw.

"Sounds like the right ground work," Peck said. He watched the young writer's pock-marked face as he talked, the pocks shifting, moving, changing places like marbles in a tight-bound bag. What Fishbein proposed was a *ten ... fifteen ... who cares? twenty-year project. I just want to do it right, do justice to it,* he said.

Peck did some simple mathematics. That would make him ... eighty-three plus!

Fishbein carried four three-ring binders that were already crammed with research. He had cassettes and microfisch and videotapes. "Only the beginning," he said grinning, looking totally mismatched in, as far as Peck could count, five patterns of tweed. "Only the beginning!"

And it was because over the next few months, Fishbein came and Fishbein went; he would appear and disappear. His truck would clatter up the Bedford drive and leave its noise in

Peck's brain. Whole new years paged by, a new decade. Peck did a remake of the *Wizard of Oz* in which the wizard travels to Kansas to ask a favor of Dorothy. Peck did *Radio Magic II* for television and wasn't happy.

A lawyer called one March announcing that an Antony Foley had bequeathed Peck ten acres of unimproved land in the interior of West Virginia. Peck said he hadn't realized West Virginia had an interior. Foley, according to the attorney, had run out of white cells—or had it been red?—he couldn't remember. At any rate, the deed was in the mail, registered. When he hung up, Peck felt curiously touched and whimsical.

Lee and Alicia had a daughter, Karmin, about the time they opened "Lee Low's San Francisco" and changed coasts. Leigh miscarried. She underwent blood tests and her doctors advised against future carrying. She called Peck and wept. He flew to Santa Fe. During her term, she had done a pastel series, *Magical Children,* and Christopher had written a long poem about his wife engendering beauty. They told Peck they had never been so close.

"I felt I was my own parents," Christopher said, "I was them—ready to be glad for me to arrive. In a strange way, I felt like I was ready to love *me,* to love *us*. Does that make sense?"

It did. Catching their grief, Peck couldn't help but break down.

They wondered if it was gone now, what they'd felt, what they'd found. "Does it leave you, Daddy?" Leigh asked. "Do you think it could be gone? Does it come back in some other way, in another form?"

Peck assured them that *absolutely,* such closeness never abdicates.

Could he guarantee it? Could he promise?

Well, ... Peck shifted, scrambled. Age and wisdom were on the line here. *Of course!* Okay, what they'd found might allude them at the moment, he understood that. At the moment they stood in, it wouldn't be apparent, and maybe it seemed like an illusion. *But, yes, of course ... guaranteed, it wasn't even a question.* Peck embraced his daughter and her bridegroom and flew home.

Jessica retired from the California bench. Peck wondered if he should sell the farm, perhaps move to where his skin itched less, to where the light came earlier in the morning and left later, to where he could call a charity to donate all his scarves. He and Jessica talked long distance about their condominium in Key West, about maybe moving there.

"I worry," Jessica said.

"About making it together?" Peck asked.

"No, that Florida is such a cliché," she said. "And about the ratio of bars to bookstores there."

They speculated about Las Vegas, about Mission Viejo, about Sedona, Arizona, and even the interior of West Virginia. Jessica said *Texas* was out of the question: "I don't like the name," she said, "it sounds like *sexist.*"

"It's two-thirds of an anagram," Peck said.

They settled, for starters, on a month in the hills of Tuscany just outside Florence. *Firenze,* Jessica kept saying and repeating, *Firenze ... Firenze,* like a voice banked by delicious foreplay. "Can Fishbein come," Peck asked, "my friend, the biographer?" then, "Only kidding."

Fishbein, nevertheless, was a sweet man for all his *dishabille.* He genuinely revered Peck. It was his honest goal to write a book equal to his estimation of subject. He wrote and rewrote

174

and triple-edited his revised draft. At the end of seven years, pieces began surfacing in respected magazines. A large chunk, a "profile," was due out in the *New Yorker* in two parts.

Fishbein came to Bedford on the day before Peck was to leave with Jessica for Italy. He wanted a final morning (his words) to triple-check his citations. They drank French roast coffee and shared a bagel. Fishbein confided he'd finally, at the age of thirty-four, fallen in love with a shy but wonderful black girl, Naomi, who worked at the New York Public Library. Would Peck and Jessica be available the following August to attend a wedding? *Yes.* Would Peck be Fishbein's best man? *Why not?* The two clamped each other with an awkward hug to show their affection, congratulations, and thanks, and then Fishbein loaded up eight boxes of film, tape, and manuscript into ICU and drove off.

Was invisibility its own trick—something hidden, and all you had to do was find it? Were there such things as omens, portents, signs, and did Peck believe in them? Did they believe in him? This is what preoccupied him a few days later, returning by his small diesel-spitting Fiat from a morning at the Uffizi, to meet Jessica at their small villa. Peck received a call from a Sergeant Henderson, New York State Highway Patrol. Did Peck know a Gerald Fishbein, he asked.

Of course.

Good, then, as Sergeant Henderson had already concluded since several of the "unobliterated items" in Gerald Fishbein's truck had borne Peck's name.

Unobliterated items? What did he mean?

Well, sorry to be the bearer of bad news, especially all the way across "the pond," but apparently Gerald Fishbein's truck, on its way from Bedford to New York, had blown a tire and spun somehow through a guard rail and plunged into a reservoir. Peck was told that, for the most part, all the tapes and films and other items in the boxes had been destroyed.

Even if one didn't believe in omens, events had a way of developing all on their own. Within a week, Peck got a second call. This time it was Punch breaking into a late meal of arista and classico chianti with news of J.T.'s liver failure.

"This isn't fair," Peck toned. "No, please." He called the news to Jessica, who wept. "Punch, I'm sorry," Peck kept saying. "Punch ... Punch, I'm sorry." Would he come? *Obviously.* Would he say something at the memorial? *Yes, of course.* Could he make J.T. appear just one more time? *That would be a tall order.*

What Peck *did* make appear was J.T.'s voice. It was his best extended impression. Those who were present laughed. They shut their eyes and let the near-channeled voice magically fill and float and fulminate. *I will never again!* ... *A dog goes into a bar with a man on a leash* ... The many people assembled from distant locations had a last glad reunion with their gruff, boisterous friend. They cried as they listened to the purrs and growls and chuckles coming from Peck, but not really *of* Peck, his vocal, vibrating chords as close an embodiment of J.T.'s voice as one could get, ranting, coaxing, and teasing. And then it was gone.

Peck found himself holding Jessica's hand like a schoolboy everywhere they went. "I'm keeping my few options as close as possible," he said.

She answered: "Finally, you've become sweet. After all this time, you've become a genuinely sweet person."

"It's always touch and go, but one hopes," Peck said.

Certain days, Peck would look at friends. He would look at the people he'd known and cared for for too long, and at the least expected of moments he'd see them as spirits rising out of their bodies, lifting, evanescing: weird prefigurations. The word *ephemeral* came into his brain like a lost fish even though he couldn't remember ever having learned it. Jessica said there could be too much life of the imagination.

Then the same thing, this dissolving and lifting, began to happen with strangers as well, people close to him in years but whom he had never known. Peck could be in an airport, a theatre lobby, a restaurant. He would see a phantom shadow, some airless silk at the hunched shoulders of a stranger, begin to shimmer at first and then drift up past his borders of vision in an ascension.

It made him shake. It made him cast back to whatever the sources for these hallucinations could be, perhaps having seen Mrs. Giarnarni in her hospital room—or was his father exercising some new talent as a spectral backdrop, a ghost? At the age of eleven, Peck made the ghost do somersaults in the air, he had made the ghost dance. Now he was seeing ghosts dance of their own.

Peck thought of Gerald Fishbein and his labor on Peck's biography. "The world is grateful," had been Fishbein's chant. "It wants to remember and feel gratitude," he had said.

Peck called the network to get their opinion on doing his own biography, which he said would be conceptualized and performed. He said he would enact some episodes from his life in three parts in a way that involved *meta-conjury*. If this held no interest for them, okay fine, have it their way; he would approach public television.

Whoa … whoa! he was told. *Who at this end of the line has raised a question?*

Peck set to work, feeling a heady empowerment flood in—swirling, eddying—filling him up and making him feel deliciously touched and visited. Nothing came to him in words, it was all vague feelings about presences and absences, appearances or vanishings, awed voyages and treks down the coastline of visibility. There were times he thought he had entirely vanished himself, left his life empty, and that he had no idea where he might have gone. There were times when *Abracadabra!* placed him inside someone else's life, someone who had arrived out of nowhere, and Peck was suddenly and undeniably, full-blown, someone else. He watched from a distance and took his own kind of notes. He watched himself the way a child sees the ace of hearts appear behind a playmate's neck, then sees it vanish at the magician's bidding to be rediscovered in the lining of some other playmate's pocket.

"Fishbein asked such extraordinary questions," Peck confessed to Jessica. "He asked, I can't think of another word, *extraordinary* questions; and most of the time, I'll plead guilty to this, I think I only half answered him."

When he presented his plan for the first of three one-hour segments of his self-portrait, which he began referring to as *My Life, Thank You*, there was an inert silence that reminded him of concrete curing slowly at a construction site. One of the network executives offered tentatively, "as obviously just, really, a point of clarification, but did you say you were going to make the town you grew up in ... *disappear?*"

"Yes," Peck said.

"I see," the executive said. "So, what then, camera cuts—we dissolve, something? I'm asking for information. I know you've done remarkable things in the past and fooled us all, but ..."

"The town disappears," Peck said. "Sometimes that happens. There are floods, whatever, acts of God, and sometimes where you grew up isn't there for a while, but it all comes back."

"From the screen, in other words. I mean, the camera cuts away to some other place, somewhere in … North Dakota, say. Disappears from the screen."

"No, from the map. It has to disappear from the map. It has to be geological—cartographical—gone from reality."

The executives eyed one another.

"But just as I said, only briefly."

"Whew!" another executive chimed. "Hate to be subpoenaed for something called Towngate!" The room laughed nervously.

"Another question," the first executive pressed.

"Yes," Peck said.

"You spoke of certain people, a number of them … close, immediate family and acquaintants, who are no longer present, who've passed on—departed—and you spoke of, … well, bringing them back."

"Yes," Peck said.

"And hey, I'm just someone with an MBA, but how do you propose to do that?"

"I can't give away my secrets," Peck said. "I'm pledged to silence."

Most of the executives moved their pens between their fingers. "Well, it sounds like, in classic form, you've got a winner here," the first executive said.

"How old are you now, Mr. Peck?" another asked.

"Sixty-eight, sixty-nine … something like that—a perfect temperature, somewhere in the high sixties."

+hirteen

Several weeks after Peck's first network meeting, Christopher called to say Leigh had been diagnosed with lymphoma. The reports were mixed; she'd begun radiation. And though Christopher's voice was clear and measured—heroic almost—Peck could hear the rupture, its brokenness rife with subterranean terror and futility. "She's doing her best work now," Christopher offered, his voice grained and piecemeal. "It's her best work." His voice spider-webbed like a struck windshield.

Though it seemed like a week, it took five years—Leigh's fading, her drifting on, her day-upon-day disembodiment—until Peck was seventy-five. Peck had postponed *My Life, Thank You* indefinitely and taken a house with Jessica in the Sangre de Cristo mountains to be nearby—to be "missionaries of whatever longevity" (Jessica's phrase). They often drove Leigh to therapy. They took, later wheeled, her into galleries. She painted on her own for over a year, standing uneasily. It *was* her best work, as Christopher had called it.

Then for nearly another year, Peck's exceptional girl, his twin daughter, painted with the help of a sling he and Christopher devised, which hung from the beams of her studio. It took her weight. It had pulleys like a clothes line, which allowed her to move laterally. Then for a time she did small, lovely watercolor studies on a pad.

Lee would fly in, sometimes with Alicia and Karmin but most times alone. He stayed in whatever room with his twin sister and stared as though trying to determine something. He could never stand still. He would appear to be about to talk, then would decide against it. He always cooked. His sister loved his food and ate all she could. "What sounds good?" he would say every morning. "I mean, for later." She would place an order. When Lee was visiting, Peck spent a great deal of time grating ginger root and being instructed in the precise butchery of duck.

For a while, for every pound that Leigh lost, Lee lost two. "See how terrible?" he would say. Then, for each of her lost pounds, he would gain. "I had it wrong," he said. "I was thinking of *sharing* when the right word was *caring*." *C'mon, Li-li, eat more,* he would say. The key concept, and he apologized for taking so long to discover it, was to keep up a robust offensive against atrophy. He lugged in all sorts of black and yellow and spotted herbs. Some of them he would make into a paste to coat his sister's skin, some got brewed like tea, and were shaved into a vaporizer tub for Leigh to inhale during her sleeping.

When Alicia and Karmin came with Lee, they seemed happy but were satellites, Alicia spending most of her time in Santa Fe. Karmin lost herself to hand puppets and drawing. Sometimes Lee would ask that nothing interrupt himself and his sister, opening a disquiet in Peck that only Lee had the ability to unlock. "What do the two of you do—sealed off for hours in your own protectorate?" Peck asked. He tried to inflect as much innocence as possible. Lee said he and Leigh remembered time spent together in their mother's womb.

After one visit, Peck, driving Lee back in silence to the Albuquerque airport, summoned the nerve and posed, "Talk is not a relaxed thing with us, is it?"

"Oh, I think it's relaxed with you," Lee said, "just not with me."

During the long journey of Leigh's fading, Christopher and his poetry coursed sometimes through violent landscapes, demonstrating rage at his center, even cruelty, confusion, self-contempt, or fear. He took a mistress for a month, then drove his Toyota into an arroyo in an absurd swipe at suicide. Peck took him out for a night apart to the Coyote Cafe. They drank, and the time, to Peck, felt briefly and strangely like some revisitation with J.T., although how to tell clearly who was who was difficult. Was Christopher a friend, and what about Leigh and Victoria? What had happened? It seemed like a replay. Was there a future and could he see what loomed? What needed to be claimed, and on which side of the drop cloth?

"Do you ever imagine asking ... as a plea bargain, sort of, to just *take her*," Peck asked Christopher.

Christopher answered by snatching up bone and gristle, tendon and meat of his remaining chicken angelina and tossing the hank past three tables, up onto a stage, where it slid to a stop in front of an oversized pink and turquoise coyote. The response had a certain of-the-moment lucidity, though it appeared lost on the management and the band that had begun to set up.

"Everyone remarks how beautiful she is," Christopher said.

"What's the worst for you?" Peck asked.

Christopher poured some more Barbara, drank it; poured again, drank. "That no words work," he said, "that my words go nowhere, that nothing changes the world I live in. Who am

I? Who's the poet and what good am I?" He hefted his glass.

"Don't throw your wine," Peck advised.

Don't throw your food! Don't throw your wine! Christopher mocked. He threw it anyway and they were asked to leave. Peck paid for the meals and breakage. Christopher took the undrained Barbara and the two drove to the hills just below Truces. "I'm thinking of joining the *Penitentes*," Christopher said. He laughed. Peck confessed himself outside the joke. They left the car to tread the moonlight. "I feel her here," Christopher said. "I feel her here so much. We'd always drive here." He broke. He hurled what he could find, pine cones, mostly, into the sky and growled. He barked and spun and threw himself to where the earth bore its dust into him. Then he lay quieted.

Peck knelt and did a trick he had nearly forgotten but had thought about recently. He produced silver balloons that materialized out of nowhere, one after the next, a hundred of them, which drifted gently up to where they changed from black to silver to gold against the eggplant hills and ivory moon.

"Lighter than air," Christopher cried.

"Deftness always, where possible," Peck advised.

"Do you carry them with you?" Christopher asked. "Do you plan it? Were they up your sleeves?"

Peck's patter was old, nearly tired after all his years. "All of a sudden," he said, "when nothing else works, *Presto!* Magic."

It was the longest vanishing Peck had ever witnessed, a sort of sawing someone in half one cell at a time. Leigh weighed a 105. She weighed 100. She weighed 98, then 97. It took four months, but Peck constructed a complex system of weights and counter weights with wires, mirrors, pastel crayons, a long posterboard that could be shuttled left and right. With the whole contraption, Leigh could work with the least strength, the lightest fingertips. "When the images stop, I'll be gone," she said. She always managed a smile. Mornings sometimes she produced breathtaking abstract diminuendos of color. *I painted my dreams,* she'd say. *See? Look, it's what I've wanted to do all my life. Now I've done it!*

For Jessica, Leigh's travail bore mixed weight. There were stretches when Jessica and Peck approached one another with gestures and words, and in pure regard for each other in ways, it seemed, that two human beings in all the ravelings of time had never done. But there were times when Peck's devotion to his daughter and his love affair with the miraculous and impossible felt like captivity to Jessica and Peck's heart appeared to be crazed and morbid.

Jessica read. Peck dug and planted gardens. She adopted two sweet and burly dogs named Search and Destroy from the Santa Fe Humane Society. During Peck's more preoccupied times, Jessica would take the dogs on mountain trails behind their home. Finally she told Peck: "I'm afraid you have business here which doesn't always include me." He protested. She said she wasn't being critical. What she'd thought to do, she said, was to periodically take trips on her own.

And she did. Sometimes she would just pack the Blazer and drive to Colorado, into Arizona, up through Utah and Idaho. Other times her trip had a plan. She'd meet a longtime friend in La Jolla or upper Michigan, Seattle. She cruised two weeks in the Caribbean.

"This is like old times," Peck said. "I commit my love, and you bolt."

"Possibly," Jessica said. She tried to smile. She kissed him and shut the trunk.

"So, what if ... I don't know, I *bite the dust* while you're off?" Peck said.

"That's not the plan," she replied. Jessica slid in and dropped her thermos onto the passenger's seat.

"What *is* the plan?" Peck asked.

"The plan is that you outlive us all," Jessica said. She closed the car door. "The plan is you outlive everybody," and she leaned through the window and kissed the tip of Peck's nose, which hovered. Then she turned on her engine. "Haven't you figured that out yet?" she asked. She smiled again and began to back out gently with Peck still leaning on the roof. "Everyone knows," she called. "Everyone! Everyone else is alert to it."

"Sounds pretty lonely," Peck said. "I don't know."

"Oh, it is pretty lonely. It's *very* lonely. But, well ..." She smiled. "You'll figure out something. You always do. You're resourceful." She gave a wave and drove off, the gravel snapping and crunching, tumbling under her four-wheel tires.

Peck imagined two scenarios. In the first, Jessica would trace a half mile of unimproved county roads, stop, burst into tears, and wonder why she allowing old patterns. She would call out *Peck! Oh, Peck!* and throw the Blazer into reverse. In just moments, they would be reunited. In the second, she wouldn't even reach the border before cracking open a pint of Jose Quervo, snapping on the radio, taking a tequila hit, and blasting with Willie Nelson: *Blue skies ... smilin' at me!* Of course, both scenarios missed the mark.

Leigh died at the far end of an April during one of her twin's visits. Peck tracked Jessica in Cody, Wyoming. She made the most sorrowful noise he had ever heard and said she would be there that evening.

Leigh's desire was for cremation, to be scattered on the mesa. Those close by came: Alicia, Karmin, Punch, certain artist friends, neighbors. Lee went to the mesa before the others and didn't return until after dark. He played music the entire time. Jessica observed him as more present and simultaneously more absent than anyone else. Peck himself felt devoid of any magic. He felt bruised, old, corrupt, wounded, unempowered. When others gathered later for simple food and wine, Peck slid out into the dusk and stood with his daughter's horse in the pasture, face pressed against the horse's flank, listening to his son's mournful memorial music. He recalled Jessica's prophecy that he would outlive them all. It seemed a questionable victory.

Christopher moved almost immediately to Europe—Portugal. He sent Peck a poem:

> She turns away, as a lily
> Stretches for light, her arm dangling
> Off the bed, her long fingers
> Curling into a fist, and reaches—
> in sleep—for the window ...
>
> Yet he remembers how
> They lashed their worn bodies
> Together by a tree, building a raft
> To float down the river,
> flowing through them to the sea.

The poem hurt Peck, it moved him deeply; he understood neither response. He and Jessica had moved back to Bedford to the farm, hoping for some ... anything, a pattern within the rooms, amidst the acreage, something they might recapture.

But what might be a pattern hid itself. It fled and darted like a rodent panic into holes, gaps, beneath stones. After a month and a half, Jessica left a note and disappeared. *Something here feels dreadfully forced,* she said. *Some beautiful ghost seems to have gone away.* She was not to be followed, she would make contact.

187

Peck opened a bottle they'd been saving, a chianti smuggled in from Tuscany. He put on Vivaldi and stood in his socks, legs spread, on the wide floorboards of his living room. *Too much light, really,* he thought, for that time of day. In one hand he held Jessica's note, in the other Christopher's poem. *So, is this what outliving everyone means? Is this the celebrated outliving process?* he wondered. *No flesh-and-blood people, just words —even from the living? Salud!* He drank.

He thought of where Jessica might have gone. He wondered if Christopher had sold the house. He remembered saying to the network, just before Leigh's ordeal, that *sometimes places disappear ... but only briefly.* He missed people. He missed places too—his room on Mott Street above Low's, the banks of the Hudson near Annandale, Leslie Fay's bathtub—but he missed the people more, those associated with these places: Victoria, Russell, Leslie. He missed his own father and their distance, he missed his mother and her heart, he missed Nicholas, he missed his uncontainable friend J.T., he missed Gerald Fishbein, he missed his angel daughter. He called Lee in San Francisco. There was no answer.

The plan is that you outlive us all.

He tried an hour later. He checked the number and tried again. The phone rang again and not even a message machine kicked in. Didn't Lee have a message machine? Of course he did. Peck tried to remember it's message, something about *perfect vegetarian lion's head, call 558-9811; for us, wait for the beep.* Which way did time go, was it earlier out west? Of course, obviously it was. The west was before ... or after, which was it? Peck thought he knew, but he felt confused. Were Lee and Alicia and Karmin still out somewhere and would be returning or had they gone to bed?

Peck called again the next morning. He called mid-morning. He called at noon. He called the restaurant. Someone named Richard passed him to someone named Lon, who passed him to someone named Michael. He was passed from reservations to the kitchen to, wherever it was, some extension to hear this Michael fellow say, "We're the new owners." How long had that been the case? Two weeks. Where was Lee? Michael said he thought Lee had moved out of state.

Where *out of state?* Peck inquired.

Somewhere out west, Michael thought.

Wasn't California *out west?*

Michael said he wasn't interested in splitting hairs. Peck asked whether they were still serving the abalone with oyster sauce. Michael said no, they'd gone nouvelle.

Peck called information. Yes, a number still showed for Lee Peck at that address. Peck kept trying. Very late, someone answered, who spoke words Peck couldn't identify. Peck kept saying *Lee Peck?* to which the far-off voice answered *Lee Peck?*

What was he to do? He called the number he had for Alicia's parents, which was no longer a working number. He tried information. No Wellington Kong existed. They had a *Priscilla* Kong. Peck called. It was, indeed, Alicia's mother at a retirement home. Wellington had been dead ten years. *Why hadn't Lee said anything?*

"Where? …"

Priscilla had trouble hearing.

Where are Alicia and Lee? Peck boomed.

Once more, please? But finally, at two in the morning, she said *New Mexico.*

Peck couldn't stop. He kept calling until he found Christopher in Portugal.

"Hey, I just got up," Christopher said.

"I'm just going to bed," Peck said.

"I'm here drinking this terrible coffee ..."

"I'm just finishing some chianti."

"... and watching the light on the water."

"I'm in the dark," Peck said. "Bulb in the hall just burned out."

"What can I do for you?" Christopher asked.

"Change places," Peck said. Christopher laughed. Peck asked whether, possibly, Lee might be leasing Leigh and Christopher's house in Santa Fe."

"He bought it!" Christopher said.

Presto-chango! Peck said.

You dance around in a ring, Christopher said.

Peck asked how he was. Had he thrown any food or wine lately? Parties. *Anything.*

Christopher said his life was bizarre, how ... fate had run. Recently he'd been ready to row a dory out into the breakers, lash on the anchor rope, and jump. But then "words started coming in," he said. "Words just ... started coming, man, like crazy. Like ... this morning: I can't get them down fast enough. I don't know. I don't know what's behind it. I don't know what's happening. I haven't met anyone ... any other person, woman or friend. But it's just gotten, I don't know, real sweet ... the last couple weeks. Rich. Have you had those feelings? Have you had those kinds of tender feelings? I want to take care of the universe. Jesus, does that sound pretentious? I'm sorry."

"After the first birth, there's all these others," Peck said.

"Hey, that's cryptic."

Peck thanked Christopher and hung up. It was three-thirty. The night was entire and deep. He tried reaching Lee and was told no such number existed. New Mexico had no listing.

The next day, Peck flew to Albuquerque and rented a car.

He drove on I-25 north to Santa Fe, his brain like a cage of agitated parakeets shimmering and squawking. The enchanted color seemed impossibly bled from light, or the light bled from the color. Peck's head ached. It ached of too much coffee, too rapid change, not enough sleep. What was it that was happening to him? What was Lee's design, and how old was he now, Lee—forty-two? forty-five? Peck's granddaughter, Karmin, would be what, almost fourteen?

With less than a mile to drive, Peck saw a familiar van, a converted blue ice-cream truck airbrushed the color of moonlight. It had been Christopher's. Beyond its windshield, Peck saw Alicia and Karmin. He leaned on his horn and waved them over. Alicia looked frightened, but she stopped and got out to meet Peck by the road's shoulder. Even through the van's tinted glass side panes, Peck could see it packed high with belongings.

"What's going on?" Peck took Alicia's hands.

She was trembling, unsteady, and biting at her lips. She took a breath. Lee had sold Lee Low's, all of them, east and west. He'd come here, he'd announced, to complete his twin's painting, finish all her images, however long it took.

Peck confessed he hadn't known Lee painted.

He hadn't, Alicia said, *until now*. He rarely slept, he stayed in Leigh's studio and ate rarely. "The work is crazy," she said. "It's mad. It isn't anything. He says only he knows what it is. Only *he* knows what it means and why it's important. I tried to get him to see someone. I brought doctors out. He locked the doors. He attacked them, threw things, screamed. That's why we're leaving. I can't stay with him."

Her shoulders shook and she sobbed openly. Peck asked that she come back and let him try to help. She shrieked *No!* Peck understood. He reached to write her a check, but she said that wasn't a problem. She had money. Lee always left the managing to her. So, where were she and her daughter headed? She wouldn't say. She did promise to call once they'd located. She called to Karmin, "Come give your grandfather a hug!" Karmin stepped out of the van and Peck noticed she was veined through with the first touches of *woman*. He nearly gasped.

"It's not good, Grampa Peck," she told him. "Will you help us? Will you make whatever it is go away?"

Peck drew her in. When he shut his eyes, all the memories began to knit and wriggle like worms. It was impossible to know where he stood, beside what road, or how old, or precisely what it was he felt, who the woman might be he was holding. "I'll do what I can," he promised his granddaughter.

Fourteen

here were stretched canvases everywhere. Some of them were square and immense, some in triptych arrangements, and one was two feet by at least thirty feet. There was an intense smell of linseed oil, dense and choking. It was hard to tell whether Lee wore clothes; he was plastered with oil paint and held what Peck later discovered was a horse's tail bought from a dog food cannery. On the floor were more than a dozen palettes, each heaped with a single color.

Music played, sounds that were either plucked or percussive. Lee dipped the horsetail into a color, then danced, spun and turned until the inspired moment when he would reach and graze multiple canvases. It looked like some ritual. It looked like some lost martial art. The images made no sense, though they had a kind of beauty that seemed to conceal something on the inside. Most of the canvases had black Anasazi glyphs, gashes of red the color of dried blood. Mixed into the paint was what appeared to be sand, deep under the colored lashes and whippings.

Peck watched several hours. Lee evinced no recognition.

Peck might as well have been air, he was that absent to his son. At last, Lee bent at the waist, half bow; half out of exhaustion. Peck made no move, voiced no sound, only waited. Finally Lee began breathing more fully, then stood and turned. He looked confused. "Who are you?" he asked.

"I'm your father," Peck said.

"Do you think?" Lee inquired.

"Well, as far as I can determine," Peck said.

"What's your evidence?" Lee asked.

"Uh, ... you have a birthmark on your left shoulder," Peck said.

"Do I?" Lee said.

"No," Peck said, "but it seemed like the thing to say. It had a certain ring to it."

"Maybe I'm *your* father," Lee said.

"Be my guest," Peck offered.

"Do you believe people can make exchanges with other people?"

"All the time," Peck said.

"One life exchanging with another life ... sometimes when people don't even know it's happened."

"Absolutely."

"You sound skeptical."

"I *am* skeptical. That doesn't mean I don't entertain such notions. Whose paintings are these?" Peck asked.

"Lee Peck's," Lee said, though it was impossible to know whether he'd said *Lee* or *Leigh*.

Peck asked if they could stop sparring. Lee said he didn't know what his father meant. Peck said he looked thin. Lee agreed, he *was* thin—thinner than soup, thinner than broth— and getting thinner. Peck asked whether he'd given any thought, in all his actions, to his family, in particular his daughter. Lee scoffed and asked what Peck was talking about. He knew very well Lee couldn't have children.

Peck walked outside and stood in the New Mexico sun. There were pinion jays and nuthatches squabbling over some suet. Lee stuck his head out the studio door. He had oil colors figured on his face like war paint. "Why don't you make me disappear?" he asked.

It was a perverse question but asked, although perversely, from a center which was not irretrievable.

"Can you turn a crazy person into a sane one?"

Peck turned and walked to the car and got his luggage. Lee watched.

"You know what happened to *your* father when he moved in," Lee prodded.

Peck said nothing. He carried his bags to the house, let himself in. A person didn't build a lifetime doing the impossible only to turn his back on it at the end.

He unpacked. He called his machine in Bedford and heard Jessica's voice. "Where *are* you," it said. He changed his message so when she called it would say: "Where are *you*?"

The refrigerator had only wine and vegetables and pasta. Peck took all the vegetables from their bins. He laid them out on the kitchen butcher block where they looked cartographical, like islands and continents on a map. He picked a turnip and an endive and head of radicchio, held them up, and juggled them. He grated some carrots, cut up some eggplant and tomatoes and chili peppers, all of which he roasted and then combined with tomato sauce.

Lee entered midway and walked past him. Peck heard a shower turn on. When Lee returned, he was wearing one of his twin's housecoats. He put on some classical guitar music while

Peck poured him a glass of beaujolais. Lee thanked him. "You're a stubborn old prick," Lee said.

"Do you want to sit and enjoy your wine first or would we rather eat?" Peck asked.

"You're a stubborn old prick," Lee repeated.

"I'm a stubborn old prick," Peck said.

"Let's drink wine for a bit and then eat," Lee said.

It went like that for weeks. Lee was lucid and possessed, determined above all to keep up his fierce path and mission. Peck functioned as a marginal phantom. He cooked, picked up, wandered the edges, dropping reminders of a life larger than Lee was inhabiting at the moment, confessing his own misfires and ineptitudes in their relationship. *When you began playing music and did it in every room of the house, I never knew whether I should ... One thing I've always wanted to ask is the Chinese thing. It always seemed to me you felt more Chinese than Caucasian, and I've always wanted to ask if that's so, and if so why, and what that was to you ... It was a terrible thing I did with Fiona Garrett— heedless and hurtful ...*

Peck would try strange, oblique comments: "Don't mind me. I just come and go. I'm the understudy." Sometimes he saw that Lee heard him and paused a beat, extending a caesura of consciousness, before hurtling on. At least Lee maintained his weight, or stopped losing in any case. He dressed less in his sister's clothes. Some evenings he would seem on the brink of speaking, opening up, but instead he would say something like, "You don't know anything about cooking." Peck would say, "My ignorance is my bliss."

Sometimes, too, Lee would laugh out loud at one of Peck's

loopy non-sequiturs, then immediately pose some patent madness so Peck wouldn't mistake his laughter for contact, for close exchange or responsiveness.

Peck's message machine dialogue with Jessica continued. Over the next nearly two months, they managed:

Belmont.

Oregon?

No.

Where, then?

Vermont.

And?

What?

So?

So, what are you asking?

Why are you calling?

This is childish.

It's a second childhood. It's okay.

Lee drifted in and heard Peck changing his message. "What's okay—what second childhood?"

"Oh, nothing," Peck said. "It's a corny game I'm playing on the phone with Jessica."

"Oh, you mean my mother's replacement?" Lee said.

"Lee, that's juvenile," Peck said. He took a breath. "People don't replace anyone else. Jessica hasn't replaced your mother, and you can't replace your sister. You can wear her clothes all you want, but nobody's going to ask you to the dance. You know that, don't you? She couldn't play your music and you can't paint her paintings. Your art is in the same league as my cooking. People might not run from the room choking, but that's about the sum of it."

The air in the room, the motes of scaled and collected time, whitened, became gelid. Lee stood frozen, his eyes and then his cheekbones folding in on themselves. His jaw clenched. His lips fluttered.

"Fair is fair," Peck said. "Someone throws you an inside breaking curve straight across the plate, you swing."

Lee turned and began to leave, then turned back. "Can I have the keys to the car, Dad?" he asked. His upper lip lifted to one side. He raked a hand back through his hair.

"I think not," Peck said. "I think not, at this moment, given the circumstances."

"What circumstances?" Lee asked.

"Well, ..." Peck stretched the syllable to forestall the question.

"I'd be curious," Lee said.

"Well, I would venture to say we have an unstable situation," Peck said.

Lee reached into his pocket. "The hand is quicker than the eye, as someone told me once." He removed some keys.

"Apparently so," Peck tried.

"Apparently so," Lee echoed.

Peck asked that Lee reconsider. He posed they go for a walk, open a bottle, pick up their conversation on a more open, less confrontative plane.

"Are you scared?" Lee asked.

Peck confessed he was.

"Good," Lee said and left. He left Peck standing stiff in place, listening to the door thud, hearing the loose gravel crunch under Lee's sandaled feet, the rental car door open and shut, the engine start.

Peck wanted to yell no. He wanted to yell to please wait. He wanted to do what they do in the movies: chase the beloved, hurl himself spreadeagle on the car hood so no one could drive off. But Peck was nearly seventy-seven, his son was forty-five.

Peck could feel his scalp tighten as he heard the car pull out. He went to the shelf and drew a glass down, dropped one cube ... two, three, four ... into the glass, covered the ice with Chivas, and stood, not moving. The house, like all other houses, made sounds; they took over, they spoke, they sent their messages.

Peck didn't drink his drink, he just held it without moving at first but then caressing the glass. He thought he should call someone, but who? Who were living still, and who were the dead? Of the living, who was nearby enough for reaching? Maybe he was overreacting, but he could imagine ragged scenes of implosion and spilled blood, fire and wreckage, his car mid-air off some mountain curve, hitting the rocky desert in a fireball. He had tried, hadn't he, to help—to do the trick, to make the cat ride the tricycle, to exchange the Atlantic and Pacific, to make the ghost dance?

For the second time in Peck's memory, he was awakened from his dreams by the apprehension of fire. There was a crazy light on his walls. Through the window, he could see Lee in the apple orchard, scaling canvasses onto a bonfire. Sparks and ashes broadcast themselves into the night sky. Christopher's old stocky horse stood near, looking on, seeming ageless, seeming wise and curious and, in his coal-red eyes, as though he'd seen such fires and such undoings for a million years. Peck broke down at the realization of Lee's safe return. He vomited in the toilet, dressed, and walked outside. Lee saw him but said nothing, simply went about his intended immolations.

"I'm not an art critic," Peck finally said. "I'm just a half-assed entertainer who worked his way up from clubs in Hoboken. Maybe you should get a second opinion."

Lee said nothing.

The two stayed on together nearly three months. At first,

they continued their relationship of nearly absolute silence. Lee wasn't insane, but he remained humorless. He worked essentially as a carpenter, fixing up and setting straight any disrepair on the property and in the house. He told his father simply that he would cook, and did. Peck accepted that. Stripped of his own caretaking jobs, Peck accepted the silence for a time, then simply talked, reflecting on his own years of folly and joy and frustration, fury at times. He tried to keep his voice close to silence—level, soft, reflective—without judgment or any agenda of teaching a lesson.

Lee occupied himself steadily, but it seemed most times he heard what his father said. Sometimes he turned up a radio or started singing to himself, at which Peck would stop. More and more, they practiced at first and then learned a conversation style that was in the present tense, never speculative or reflective. It would go *I think my hair's finally falling out* or *Look at that cedar waxwing* or *When I'm fixing the stable door today, I discover the hinges are hand-made. They've been struck in a forge.*

Peck found Alicia and got in touch with her. He said Lee was on the mend. He'd bought a restaurant space in Santa Fe and was preparing it. Alicia cried. Karmin got on the phone and cried. Peck advised them to wait until Lee called for them, but he suspected it would be soon. The next day Lee asked, "Do you know where my wife and child are?" A week later the family reunited and Peck decided to leave. As Lee deposited Peck's bags into his trunk, he said, "I guess it's not just fathers who can be assholes."

All Peck could do was laugh. No snappy rejoinder came to mind. He hooted. "Oh dear, oh dear!" he cawed. He said it again and again, bent over, crumpled.

"Are you all right, Grampa?" Karmin asked, seeing this from the yard and running close.

Peck couldn't answer. He just laughed. Lee began to catch the fever and started in. Peck fell against the car onto the ground. Lee toppled over, nearly falling on top of the old man, their bodies slipping together like lovers. They began to wrestle, laughing and rolling with each other.

"Mom! Mom, come quick!" Karmin yelled from standing above. Alicia burst into the front door frame of the house.

"We're fine!" Peck comforted, laughing and rolling still. "We're fine! This is good. This is a *very* good thing."

Peck found Jessica on Hilton Head Island. Her younger brother, seventy-two, lived there in a retirement home. "Let's check in, too," Jessica said, "and leave the cooking to them—to you know, them who can."

"I can still cook," Peck insisted, "just not very well." He greeted Robert, the brother. Robert studied Peck. He'd been the welcoming doorman on Peck's capsized dates with Jessica in high school and had gone on to teach theater at a university. He brushed his silver hair straight back. They'd met various times. "What're your acting plans?" Robert asked.

Peck said his plans were to continue acting.

"When's your season?" Robert asked.

"Winter," Peck said.

"He meant your *theatrical* season," Jessica prompted.

"I know," Peck said.

They had a halting, oblique discussion about actors and acting styles. Robert's sense of the present seemed to shuttle between sometimes very good and other times completely confused. When Peck begged their departure, Robert asked if he planned to tamper with the text.

"As much as possible," Peck said.

Robert said he always tried to honor the text, and Peck

confessed this was probably the difference between them.

On the drive back to Bedford, Jessica apologized for her skittishness, her disappearance from Santa Fe and her flight. She said that when situations got shadowed and dubious, that was her typical response. It's an old story, she said.

Peck drew her in and said, "We're an old story," repeating "old" several times. The two of them laughed. "But I keep reading that old story," he said. "It's one I like."

The next two and a half years were sweet ones with the farm as a base camp. All the bulletins from New Mexico spelled regeneration. Lee and Alicia were newly happy. The restaurant, called Leigh's, was thriving. Karmin was to have a brother; ultrasound spilled the beans. Alicia had set up a decorating business that was thriving.

Peck refused work. He refused to endorse products. His network producers pressed him, saying he couldn't just keep putting off *My Life, Thank You.* "We've announced it just as you specified as a three-part project," they said.

Peck responded that he was doing "retirement living," that he'd meant to years ago but was too busy, so now he was getting it out of his system. He told his producers they shouldn't worry, he'd come raging back "like a maniac."

He and Jessica traveled to wherever there was warmth, whether southern France or the coast of Mexico. Lee and Alicia called to announce the birth of Nicholas Tom Peck, saying they were thrilled. In fact, Peck was thrilled. *Nicholas Tom* was a nice name, it had a nice resonance. Lee stayed on the phone and rambled nonstop. *Oh, and ... then I was thinking ... I mean, what could be wrong ... why couldn't a person? ... Oh, and the little black turtleneck you sent for Nicholas Tom? It's too small now, but—*

Peck had never heard his son talk so much. It had never occurred to him that Lee commanded that many words in his vocabulary, never mind actually using them. "Has something happened with your speech center?" Peck asked. Lee didn't seem to get it.

"Did it ever seem to you that Thursdays were holy?" Lee went on, "that they were, when you think about it, I mean, closely, more holy than Sundays or Saturdays?" Then he'd go off on his whole theory about Thursdays as Sabbath.

All the while, something began happening with Jessica's bones. *Barnacles,* Peck diagnosed, but the doctors disagreed. *No,* they said, *it's more complicated.* All her joints had become stiff, resisting either straightening or bending, and there was more and more pain. She bore it stoically, then took Darvon, then screamed from the unbearableness of it.

She told Peck she hated him, how he was escaping such humiliation. Obviously, he knew some trick, she said. She called him Coyote, raged that he'd spent too much time in New Mexico. Why didn't he just go away!

He warmed oils and liniments and worked them into her joints. When he hit a raw, "live" area, she'd sometimes strike him, leaving a deep gash or bruise, and then cry all the worse, feeling terrible for it. Peck thought it was generally a black-and-blue time. There were achingly black stretches of very blue days and weeks.

Jessica's brother, Robert, died—of *triteness,* Peck thought, from being old, scattered, disabled—when he fell and broke his hip and then departed a day later. Jessica couldn't collect her own body enough to go to him and blamed herself.

In Peck's sleep at night, after Robert's death, Jessica's image came to him, her face framed in a car window: *You're going to outlive us all,* she said, but this wasn't the end of the dream. She went on, saying: *You're going to appear and appear and appear while the stage empties.* Peck waked up drenched in a sweat, his chest feeling pummeled, the FM station he'd fallen asleep to playing something like Mahler. He *hated* his good fortune, he thought. He was now eighty.

Once a week like clockwork, polaroid shots of Nicholas Tom arrived from Taos: Nicholas Tom propped in pillow, Nicholas Tom situated under a mobile with eyes wide open, Nicholas Tom doing possibly his first push-up, Nicholas Tom on the other side of a window.

Jessica kept to her own room. Peck bought her a walker, which she pushed down the stairs and struggled with back to the room she'd claimed. Peck bought a wheelchair and she locked its brakes and wouldn't move. He put a motor on the wheelchair and she jammed a wire coat hanger into the motor and shorted it, mildly electrocuting herself. She told Peck she felt better and that the voltage had lubricated her joints.

During one dinnertime, Peck was doing the best he could in the kitchen when he heard something on the stairs. Jessica was marshaling herself, bend by bend, extension by extension, and was descending. "If I can electrocute myself every couple of days, I might be fine," she said. In fact, her spirit rose for a day or two.

But then it sank. A week later, she tried another coat hanger in an electrical outlet. Peck smelled burned hair and went to investigate. Jessica's eyes looked like the yolks of eggs. She was dazed and shaking. That night, once again, she walked downstairs, calling over the balustrade, "I'd like a whiskey sour." Peck felt there were dangerous precedents being established and stripped her room of anything metal she might attempt to use for rejuvenation.

What Peck took in with Jessica was a new perversity that filtered, perhaps as an act of sharing love, into his own professional life. The next time he got a call to film an endorsement, this one for the classiest new edition of Ford Motors, he said yes. The idea behind his participation was that he was an entertainer whose spirit and drive defied all wear, who "stood up" and "kept going," just like a Ford. The plan was to have him sit in a director's chair beside the car and utter some kind of wise and pithy endorsement. He would bank two hundred thousand for the appearance.

The set was dressed and finished. All the light readings and voice levels were in place. Peck was in his trailer when he received the call to take his place in his chair. The director looked around. "Where's the car?" he asked. The car's taped marks were on the set. It had been backstage and was to be driven in. No one knew where it was. The question, *Where's the car?* caromed the interior like a banked billiard shot. Finally the producer of the ad and the director came to Peck. "The car's disappeared," they said. "Our Ford."

"It happens," Peck said.

"Fine, okay. We understand you're the magician. But if you would just tell us *how* it happens."

"Magic," Peck said.

They called a dealership. They had an identical model sent over. Peck sent out for angel-hair pasta. The car was driven onto the set. Studio guards were stationed in the wings. They shot the ad, five takes before they called it a wrap. Peck was wry and wonderful, they said, until they viewed the takes for editing. Although Peck was still wry and wonderful, the car wasn't in the shot. Clever, the producer had to admit. Brilliant, even, perhaps. But—"

Where'd it go? they asked Peck. Peck shook his head. "It

was here," they said. "It was in the frame and on the monitor. How did it disappear off the tape?"

"These are mysteries," Peck said, "mysteries of the universe. Some of them are indecipherable."

Ford Motors threatened to withhold pay. Peck swung a platoon of lawyers in and forced the issue. Within a week, he banked his check.

When he got asked about *My Life, Thank You,* his emphatic vote was to wait. Make preparations, but wait. Film it when his life was over, then it could be complete. A younger, humorless producer tried to argue, but the man's youth and lack of humor, his argumentative strain, served only as an intoxicant to Peck. It was like a spring day. It was a picnic!

Peck played hide-and-seek with the man, putting his hands up to his face, spreading his fingers, closing them, taking them away, putting them back, taking them away again. "Boo!" he said to the man. "Boo!"

"Now listen here!" the young producer began.

"Hey!" Peck screamed. "Now hey!" Then he smiled. "Wait," he whispered, "wait."

They both waited.

Peck rocked his head like a metronome. Then he started to chant. *My life is my life. You don't understand, my life is my life.* He kept saying it like it was a Buddhist mantra. The young producer didn't have a clue, kept trying to break in to *beg to differ* and *be reasonable* and point out why it was irrelevant in this case. "No, Socrates," Peck kept saying; "No, Socrates, *you* don't understand—it's my life."

The weekly archives of bulletins and Polaroids from Taos didn't stop. Nicholas Tom was swimming, the news came. At only four, he was swimming! He was beginning gymnastics!

Peck read back through his saved packets of cards and photos and letters, unable to remember, precisely, the walking news. Had he missed it? How and when had the toddler begun to walk? At four, Nicholas Tom would probably be doing that, the walking; this would be the case, wouldn't it? People didn't swim before they walked, did they? Amphibious types might, but *people* people didn't.

A real estate conglomerate in Florida hired Peck to film an ad promoting a luxury retirement community near Tampa. The pitch was that Peck would sit in a model apartment with a tapestry fabric, high pile, brass and glass design. Peck would look up, smile, say something warm and witty about the "harvest years" and "aging wine," then the ad would cut to shots of fine dining, oil painting classes, and shuffleboard.

The local director had heard about Peck's recent "difficulties" and forwarded the notion of advance-hyping the event in the newspaper, then film the ad live. His thought Peck would not be able to sabotage live work.

They flew Peck down, got him a lavish suite, told him *relax in the sun* until everything on the set had been double-checked and was ready. They'd send a limo and do two, possibly three run throughs before the live shooting. It would take "twenty minutes max" out of his life.

It all happened just as outlined, but when the live shoot rolled with millions of viewers tuned in, everyone focused on a mysteriously slow-moving truck that encroached on the scene as Peck began his witty and warm commendation, suddenly an enormous wave of water swept through the studio, swirling furniture and sound and video equipment … left … right … off the sound stage, eddying everything.

When the water had gone and people were lifting themselves out of the silt and mud, Peck said, *Jesus! I recognize that wave. It's from the Noah's ark picture we shot fifteen years ago!*

Karmin sent Peck a telegram. She'd been accepted into the acting program at Juilliard, that's how much she was *his* granddaughter.

Peck celebrated his eighty-first birthday moving Jessica into a home. She had almost no movement left in her limbs and needed more help than Peck could render. He sat with her at the home where his father had been, Leander Manor, rehearsing the infinite ways and years he had loved her. He set drops into her eyes so her lids could move. He kissed her wrists, nibbled her elbows, and her chin. He imagined she was trying to smile. When he left her at dusk, he broke down in his car and shouted and bawled all the way, unable to stop through dinner, feeling the vastness of the loss, the inequity. He raged and shouted and cried through a late uneasy sleep. When Jessica died two and a half months later by somehow clutching a hair drier with one hand and touching the metal sole of a shoe to some spilled water, Peck was done. He was spent; he had all his grieving over with.

He felt he couldn't stay at the farm. He wanted to be where there was more life than he could bear. He packed up and flew to Hong Kong, rented a small flat, and walked the streets. Everything was vertically oriented in the city, and as he looked up, he could see scenes from his past hovering just barely over his head. He could see Russell in a café, playing guitar, J.T. having trapped some wide-eyed girl against a building, telling her all the reasons she should love him. And there, on a street corner, were Tyrone and Chad and Louis gathering a crowd for Theater of Monte. Of course, Victoria, his children's mother, was everywhere defying gravity like a dancer on stage.

Months later, back in the States, Peck agreed to play a role in a movie. It was about two runaway kids hooking up with an eighty-six-year-old man. *That's three years off,* Peck said. *I'll need makeup.* The two decide to abduct the man from his ramshackle home near Phoenix and take him on the road, where they form a kind of family. *Truants,* it was called, and Peck liked it. He liked the idea that a man in his eighties might hook up and run with teenagers. It seemed like it was just, if not appropriate. But he didn't like the end when the old man's mind begins to quaver like dust. Peck played this part through tears, which the critics found to be incredibly authentic. Peck was "hot again," and the film was a hit. More scripts arrived in the mail. New requests came in from writers who wanted to pick Peck's mind, author his biography. Meetings about *My Life, Thank You* took on a new urgency.

To break the continuum, or to imagine that he had, Peck moved to Key West. Most days, he hired a local to take him out onto the water, where he would sit on the deck of a thirty-foot boat reading mystery novels, watching pelicans. Or he would walk the length of Whitehead Street, stroll the city beach, pick up driftwood and shells, go for lunch at the Half Shell and eat oysters and drink dark rum.

Often in the evenings he'd meander through Mallory Square to see the sunset. One night a nineteen-year-old introduced herself as Tricia Spaulding and announced she was in love with him and might they marry? She had *always* been in love with him, she said. *Always?* Peck said, and Tricia Spaulding said, *Yes, certainly so.* Peck said he could never marry someone who measured time differently, but if it would make her feel better, he'd be happy to saw her in half. She walked away fuming. Peck thought of Fiona Garrett for the first time in many years. He thought of how nice it would be, measurements of time aside, to spend one more fevered evening with such a creature.

Nicholas Tom was selected for a regional all-star soccer team. The team played a team from Mexico City, so Peck flew in to see the game. Nicholas scored the winning goal in the second overtime. There was a post-game photo in *Sports Illustrated* of Nicholas on Peck's shoulders. The caption read "Face of the future, face of the past."

Peck did a television ad for a brokerage firm. No tricks this time. No perversity. His opening line was, "You don't know how much pleasure it gives me to say the word *securities.*" About that time, someone brought out an unauthorized Peck biography. Peck took space in the *New York Times Book Review* to respond with: "This is the best book ever written about me by a child abuser." When told the writer was initiating a suit, Peck announced that the statement in the ad had come from *another Peck,* the one in the man's unauthorized biography.

A call came from granddaughter Karmin, out of Juilliard and opening in her first equity production, *Mother Courage,* in San Diego. Would Peck come? *Would he come! Of course, how could he not?*

"Are you Mother Courage?" he asked.

"I'm too young," she said.

"Karmin, remember this: you are never too young or too old."

In fact, she was playing a mute girl, Karmin said, without any lines but a lot to do. She said she hoped that Peck wouldn't be disappointed.

"How old am I?" Peck asked her, the question arriving involuntarily from head to lips, as questions did from him these days. *Eighty-five?* she guessed. "I think more," Peck said. "I think more than that. I think I may be getting up there."

After the opening, Peck took his family—Lee, Karmin, Alicia, and Nicholas Tom—out for chenin blanc and calamari. "Is the sky here always filled with airplanes?" he asked Karmin. She said she hadn't noticed. Another couple at the restaurant ventured by the table: *You were wonderful* they said to Karmin, breathlessly echoing one another. *You were so sad, so clear, so intense.* Then they turned to Peck. *Hello,* they said politely.

Peck got restless in Key West and moved to San Antonio. He got restless in San Antonio and moved to Manhattan Beach. What he was looking for, he said, was that certain light and a place where the light arrived by seven at the latest each morning and never left before six, like the light sometimes in the Greek Islands except more like New Mexico. He moved to Las Vegas, where one could find, at any hour, any amount of light one wanted. Caesar's Palace shrugged and asked Peck if, since after all, he'd moved into town, he would sign an exclusive contract. Peck said, *Yes, thank you, and might I please have a ten-year contract?* He was eighty-eight. Caesar's obliged. Every three months, as the contract stipulated, Peck did five days of work.

During one of his shows, he made a craps table in the Olympic Casino disappear. People gasped, jaws dropped, and corporate wasn't at all pleased because, at the instant of the disappearance, a high roller had been rolling the dice. *Seven out!* the dealer said. "I just did a trick," Peck told his overflow showroom audience, "which you didn't see. It was a vanishing trick, which is a trick in itself. But when you get out into the casino afterwards, ask about it."

At the midnight show, he brought the table back, knocking down a pit boss but otherwise elegant in its effect. Another night, two of the outside fountains vanished and the middle of Fremont Street downtown suddenly flooded, where at first the city thought they had a burst a water main. *The guy's still good, but he's getting senile,* the chief entertainment executive at Caesar's said.

Peck got restless in Las Vegas and spent seven months in Spain. The light there was nearly perfect, but he couldn't digest the food. He moved back to Key West.

Peck was shocked to hear that his son Lee had died suddenly in a freak event in the desert in New Mexico. Lee was fifty-eight. The details of exactly what may have happened jockeyed crazily for position. It was known that Lee loved to hike. He loved the ancient and the native cultures—their mysteries and ruins—and had headed off on a Monday to visit Bandelier, the excavation of kivas and dwellings near Los Alamos.

That evening, three hours past dark, Lee had neither been seen nor heard from, so Alicia called the state police. There had not been any reported vehicle collisions or deaths, and Lee's red Subaru wasn't in the Bandelier lot. Then just before four, the sky still thick and haunted, the car was found off the road, shrouded by aspen, in the Bandelier vicinity. Lee wasn't inside. With daylight, a search began, and by noon a low-sweeping helicopter spotted a queerly reclined figure near Painted Cave.

It was Lee, lifeless, with blisters across his full body. Tests showed no other external injuries besides what appeared to be chemical burns. Whatever had burned his skin caused trauma to his eyes, and it was speculated that he may have been blinded before the time of death. The police said there were indications his body had been *moved* to the discovery site but that they couldn't speak conclusively.

"Then, what is it exactly you're saying?" Peck, who had flown in immediately, asked the coroner.

"I'm saying it appears to have been an encounter," the coroner said, "with some kind of massive energy source that produced an immense amount of heat or light."

Encounter with ... energy source ... immense heat or light. Alicia said she didn't want to hear such words. "I just want to know how it happened!" she said. "I just need to know what happened to my husband."

The attendant coroner and enforcement authorities opened and shut their mouths, turned their wrists to display helpless hands, palms upward. They had no answer, and if they could speak candidly, the chances were there would not be any answers forthcoming.

Had Lee hiked too long in direct sunlight? Had he ingested some savage desert plant, thinking it benign? Were there creatures whose venom was that toxic and searing? What were the potential risks to human beings in such places?

Peck asked for an investigation, though his sense was that no one would be able to determine a clearer cause. *How was it done?* Alicia had asked. *I don't want to hear about heat and light. How was it done?*

It was, of course, a question Peck had heard and asked nearly all his life. Even though at the right times not knowing could be a wonderful rainbow net, it could never heal once the pain had come. Sometimes you just had to release balloons or make the ghost dance; but try as you might, you could never make the dead live. That was a phantom, ultimate illusion.

Peck remained nearly a month, wanting to make a difference somehow in the sadness, but he was not Alicia's husband or Karmin and Nicholas Tom's father. He was just a person in the way.

He was a meager presence, really, and really no one's closest of kin anymore. Not at ninety. More realistically, he was just a very old man, just a very, very old man who had managed what the alarming Jessica had said he would do in outliving them all. Yes, he had outlived them and was now as he had begun, alone—by himself, on the edges of things.

"Stay with us, live with us," Alicia said at the end of his time.

Peck was stunned. He declined. "I have to decline," he said, and laughed unsettlingly, too giddy at his own pun.

"It would make us happy," Alicia said.

Peck shook his head. He cried. He stood and laughed. He excused himself and went to his room and stared at his return plane ticket. Could he trick his own sense of the truth? Was there a sleight of hand to make such a ticket unavailable?

At last, Peck filmed *My Life, Thank You*. The time seemed right. He requested one segment only, three being beside the point and softening the metaphor. "You arrive at a point where what is important is what's refused in dying," he said.

The producers asked what he would need, specifically, for the taping, and Peck said only more brain cells. When it came time for the show, he perched on a stool, center stage, with a live audience, looking impish. He talked and simply remembered. There were no props. The space was stripped bare to its basic grid and lighting to the back walls. "Nothing up my sleeves," Peck said, "nothing in the wings, exactly."

He recalled, he mused and drifted. Scenes would appear suddenly. A steamer trunk on a rug. Balloons rising. A woman with her back to the audience in a bathtub. A toy tricycle and three cats. Sudden guitar music. Infant cries from a delivery room. A lit and decorated Christmas tree. A human figure on fire. A wheelchair which glowed electrically. The images came and went. They appeared and disappeared. Faces floated up like dreamy holograms into the air, then faded. The room that was the theater grew pungent with Chinese cooking. The words of poems, the words of songs, clips from films, the images of paintings, the sound of wind, of water, a certain light. Everything came in its time and went as Peck remembered, and no one in the audience made a sound.

It was curious, as Peck had for years now kept asking himself if he *felt* old … or even older. What was it like? What were the differences? He moved with less precision, that was true, but he still, on most occasions, felt graceful; he sensed a center within the lesser weight and machinery of his body. And too, the world and its images seemed more granular. He desired less, believed more. Certainly more slipped into whatever might be the void than appeared from it. More went than came. Still, he felt closer than ever, it seemed, to certain secrets—not so much to what they were but where they existed. And there was an almost unsettling ferocity in that.

After the television special, he began to revisit as many places as he could: his town, their street, the house. There was a new school where he had first danced with Jessica. Antony Foley's house had been painted grey. Peck walked the streets of Boston, some of them unchanged, some gone or built over. He walked the wards of his father's hospital, and it seemed the same patients were attached to the same bottles and tubes: the same people's lives hung in the balance, some to return like Mrs. Giarnarni and some to vanish elsewhere. He flew to New York and wandered Mott and Pell streets, stood in front of the carts of shrimp and sea bass. On an early morning, he drifted along Canal Street and visited the building where Kelson Kopf's office had been. He went to Hoboken to find there was no more PussKat Club. He stood outside brownstones where J.T. had torn down walls and made thousands of dollars. In a condemned building, he walked up the broken stairs which had

215

led to his and Victoria's apartment. He flew to Corfu and walked the old town. He stood at the waterfront. He flew to Minnesota and took a room in a motel near where he and his father had stayed when they checked his mother into treatment. He flew to Las Vegas. He flew to Florence and drove a Fiat up into the Tuscany hills where he had been briefly but oh-so-sweetly with Jessica. He flew to Santa Fe. Then he flew back to New York, and back to Santa Fe, and to Key West, where he stood one last time on the pier and watched the sunset. He flew a third and final time to Santa Fe. When all his revisiting was done, when he was ninety-three, he flew back to New York and took the train to Bedford to reopen the farmhouse and stay there to die.

Biographers still chased him. He got offers for shows. Dear, dear Alicia called periodically, hoping for Peck's reconsideration of living with her. *Are you managing? Does someone come in when you need help?* A film festival in Park City called. They wanted to honor him for what they called his lifetime achievement. Would he put in an appearance. Well, an *appearance* might be fun, Peck said; watch for him, but he really couldn't be there in the flesh.

It was a May Thursday and deceptively warm when Peck had lain briefly, enjoying the robins and finches, in the bed he had shared with Victoria and then Jessica. He had risen, shaved, gotten irritated at how often now he cut himself. He had had his usual breakfast of oatmeal and whole wheat toast and had gone for a walk. He had been ninety-four now for seven months. Most times life seemed so thrilling to him, just that life had been given to him, that he'd had it, he might be standing in the open air and would feel a shiver, a kind of welling, just to think of it.

On this day he began to weep tears of enormous gratitude.

And so, when a different shiver came when he was standing in the orchard, taking in the new spring of whatever year it might have been, he could only give in to it. He could only reach out and say, *Yes, this is fine, thank you.* He could only cherish the fate that was his. That was all the sentiment that was left in him: cherishing what time he had had and feeling grateful for it. He could only say *Yes* and *Here I am.* And finally, he could feel himself slipping away and disappearing. He could feel himself, finally, gone.